Are
We
Lucky Yet?

Other Books by Jane Bradley

Power Lines and Other Stories

Living Doll

Are We Lucky Yet?

Stories by

Jane Bradley

Press 53
Winston-Salem

Press 53

PO Box 30314

Winston-Salem, NC 27130

First Edition

Cover design by Kevin Watson

Hand-knitted letters by Susan Falco

"A Long Way From Derbyshire" in *XX Eccentric*; "The Amish Man" and "Calypso" in *Cimarron Review*; "A Taste of Gianni Mascarpone, Please" in *MOTA: Integrity* and in *Sex and Chocolate*; "Lost Souls Go Wandering" in *Confrontation*; and "Are We Lucky Yet?" in *Imagination and Place*.

Printed on acid-free paper

ISBN 978-0-9825760-0-7

To my sister, Susan

Contents

A Long
Way
From
Derbyshire

He hadn't touched her yet, but she knew he wanted to. She could tell by the way he had kept his eyes on her in the restaurant, watched as she dipped her fork in the *fungi crostini*, spread the mixture of mushroom, garlic and cream on the toasted bread tip. He had leaned forward, just a little, when she raised the bite to her mouth. As she swallowed, his gaze followed the movement of muscle down her throat. He took a swig of his beer and asked if it was good. She had said yes, even though the sauce was too thick, almost gelatinous in the way it held the mushrooms in a clump on her fork. He had laughed, said, no it isn't. I can tell by the way you eat. She couldn't lie. So she shrugged and said it was normally a dish she liked.

1

Minutes later he grabbed her plate and talked her into eating his steak. She had resisted a little, but ate it, a lovely rare filet topped with gorgonzola. He nodded and smiled while she ate his steak, and she'd had this little rush of a feeling that between bites a deal had been made.

Now she was considering what else he had seen about her while watching her eat. She was wondering how she would respond when he touched her, when the red neon sign of the Belladonna restaurant behind them flickered, went out. Once again she had closed down a place, sipped the dregs of her wine as the busboy vacuumed carpet and the bartender handed off the night's profits to the manager who had given them that look—*get on with it you two, it's time to go*. Now she stood silently under the awning and wished the man she barely knew would say something, because after all the usual middle-age first dinner date conversation of marriage and divorce, and children or not, and moving for job options and retirement plans, she had run out of words. The parking lot stretched out before them under a dull night sky, and a fog sat like wet gauze over the lights of the sporadic traffic going by. The fast food signs down the street grew blurrier, seemed to move farther away as the fog thickened to a mist.

She could hear him breathing. She glanced around, saw that all the shops of the strip mall were closed. "I didn't know it was so late," she said, the stock phrase hanging in the air like a burp, barely noticed, politely overlooked. She wished she could summon up some witty banter as Lizzy Bennet certainly would have done while verbally sparring with Mr. Darcy in *Pride and Prejudice*. But Longbourne and Netherfield were just fanciful places where the protagonist walked purposely through muddy fields to sort her troubles out, where she possessed the patience and wit, and integrity required to get the happy ending. But that was another world.

Twice divorced and resigned to a new job in the industrial wasteland of Northwest Ohio, Hope was long past what most considered a marriageable age. Here I am, she thought, a new city, a new job, and new potential man for my bed, but all she could manage to feel was smudged once again from too much talk, too much listening, and too much wine. She looked out at her Camry and his SUV, like pets waiting in the dark for their masters to claim them, take them home. They looked alone, forlorn somehow in the otherwise empty parking lot. She gave a hard little sigh. It would be a long walk in the high-heels that were already burning her toes.

"You all right?" he said.

"Sorry," she said. I was just thinking."

The mist turned to rain with a whooshing sound.

"What were you thinking?"

She could smell his cologne that reminded her of streams, and trees, and cold clear air. "I was thinking how I'd get to my car in the rain."

"No, you weren't thinking that." He nodded toward a wrought iron bench behind them. "We can sit back there until the rain passes."

She followed him. "I was really wondering if this night were a story, how would it end."

"If it were my story, the main character, he'd end up getting laid."

The rain made a steady thrumming sound. She breathed the smell of rain on pavement, the mildly acrid scent of asphalt. After awhile, if rain kept coming the air would turn sweeter, clean. "But it's my story," she said.

"Really." He tugged at her arm, pulled her further back under the awning. She liked the way he wiped the bench first with his handkerchief. She sat, relieved.

He pulled a cigar from his pocket. "Do you mind?"

"Go ahead," she said.

He clipped the cigar, lit, inhaled and looked out at the lot as if it were his own yard and he could just sit back and watch it rain all night.

His name was Mike. A mechanic's name, she thought, like Joe or Frank, a name for a man who took things apart with his hands. She had watched him at parties, in restaurants, at her gym. She knew he was somewhat dangerous with his way of quietly possessing a room when he entered, pausing to let his thick muscled presence sink into position, lifting his head slightly like a lion sniffing the wind for prey. But she liked that animal kind of thing in a man. There was a time when she was hungry too, going through men like meals, carefully chosen, savored, swallowed, then gone to the realm of memories: *remember that night when we had . . . oh yes. . . it was good.*

He blew his smoke above them, looked at her, grinned. "Did you like my steak?"

"You know I did. I ate all of it."

"I liked watching you eat," he said. "You eat like a kitten, such fierce and hungry little bites."

She felt herself blushing. "Nice metaphor," she said. "Where'd a contractor learn to talk like that?"

"Where'd a professor learn to eat like that?"

"It's a primal thing." She liked the word primal, the way it upped the ante in any conversation with a man.

"Mm, hmm." He grinned, gave a quick little nod as if he'd checked off a point. She heard his cell phone vibrate in his pocket and watched as he checked the caller. "My son," he said. He listened then went on to view the other calls missed.

He was a handsome man, big and broad with thick graying hair and a well-trimmed beard, and blue, blue eyes that sparked like a lit fuse ready to explode. In spite of all his talk, she didn't really know him, just she knew of him:

a man who bought properties and with a little dry wall and plumbing and paint turned ruin into gold. They said he had the Midas touch. Yes, she thought, he looked like a man who could have been a greedy troubled king, who wielded thick swords, bedded pretty women, and fed freshly killed deer to his dogs. He snapped his phone shut, shoved it in his pocket and gave her a smile. She had heard he collected women like those distressed properties he bought and sold, and now his appraising eye had settled on her.

She looked out at a parking lot dimly lit by a security light far away where the pavement gave way to scrubby grass and a line of trees. And there at the far corner of the lot by the street was a boat, a luxury boat all white and chrome and sitting there like something marooned. She hadn't noticed it when she pulled in, her mind preoccupied with how she looked, with whether he'd be waiting for her at the bar. She nudged his arm. "Why is a boat sitting out there in a parking lot? We're nowhere near a marina."

"It's the Commander," Mike said. He looked out at the boat as if any moment it could rev to life and take off. "It's got an inboard V8. Goes up to fifty miles an hour, can take rapids and streams only four inches deep. Got a power to weight ratio you wouldn't believe."

"Why is it sitting in a parking lot?"

"Promotional," he said. He nodded toward the plate glass window of the tobacco shop behind them. "They sell high end fishing gear along with those cigars."

She stood up and peered in through the dark glass of the storefront. In the dull electric glow of the display cases she could see leather wing back chairs, some chess boards, taxidermy fish placed on shelves, a deer head on the wall and something like a fox, she thought, in the corner. "Pretty pretentious."

"It's just good cigars and good gear." He put his hand on her shoulder, turned her back toward the parking lot. "Come summer they give fly fishing lessons out there."

"On pavement?" she said. "People stand out there and cast in a parking lot."

"It's one way to learn." He stood with his arms crossed over his chest and studied the boat with that way men have of looking at a job to be done.

"Desperate people in desolate places," she said.

He shook his head, walked away from her. "I grew up here. It's not a bad place to live."

"I'm sorry. I didn't mean that."

"Anybody anywhere can be desperate."

"Yeah," she said. "I know that." She looked out at the boat. "It's just back home it'd be strange to learn to fish on pavement. We've got all these lakes and rivers, and streams."

"Learning how to fly fish on pavement seems pretty resourceful to me."

"Yes, it is." She sat back on the bench, hoped he would join her, but he stood a little ways behind her, smoking.

"Wouldn't it be nice," she said, "if we could jump in that boat and crank it up and fly away."

"Boats don't fly."

"I was being metaphorical."

He sat next to her, leaned close. She could feel the soft heat of his beard on her face. "We can fly in that Range Rover of mine out there. I've got a way with engineering things."

"Not tonight," she laughed. She shifted away from his touch and stood as if to go. She thought he'd stand to stop her, but he just sat enjoying his cigar. "People at work told me that the Belladonna is where all you upscale local types go." She stopped. "You know."

"You upscale local types?" he said studying the glowing tip of his cigar.

"You know what I mean," she said.

"Yeah, I know what you mean."

She sat beside him. "I'm just saying if I were making a movie of a yuppie pick up bar, I'd show that. All the beautiful ones. Tanned and toned and groomed. The dark-haired men fondle cell phones while Botoxed blondes nod and smile. Hooking up, networking, hanging out, whatever word we use, it's just another form of sniffing, marking turf, moving in to gauge which way the power goes."

"I thought you taught literature," he said. "Is this a political science class?"

"I'm just saying," she said. She wasn't sure what she was saying.

He blew smoke above her head and smiled. "Sounds to me like you're saying you had too much to drink."

"No. Well yeah," she said. "But I'm saying it's like dogs. These rituals. When they meet at the park, their eyes lock, ears perk. Little sniffs, steps forward, back, and then off they go nipping, yapping, running circles in the grass." She sighed, wished she'd just quit talking. But she couldn't. "It's just that we like to think we're so evolved."

"You don't ever want to get laid?" Mike said.

"What?" she said.

"Laid," he said. "Don't you ever want that, professor? Instead of all this talk."

"Well of course I do."

"Good," he said.

"So," she said.

"So."

"Well," she said when she saw the pulsing yellow light of the security guard's truck turn into the parking lot. He was heading their way. "Guess he's making the final rounds. Must be time to go."

The guard slowed in front of them, gave Mike a smile and a thumbs up sign. Then he turned away.

"He knows me," Mike said. "This place, it's like my neighborhood bar."

The guard flicked off the flashing light on top of his truck, sped up and headed for the exit. He darted across the street and pulled quick and sharp into the Taco Bell.

"I thought cops preferred diners and doughnuts."

"He's not a cop, just a guard they hire to make the place look watched over."

"I see he's really good at his job."

Mike shrugged. "He's got a girlfriend at the Taco Bell. She's married, he's married. So they meet there, have a quickie on her breaks and when she gets off."

"In that little truck."

"In that little truck." Mike grinned. "He says she's very flexible."

Mike threw his cigar to the ground and moved closer to her.

"How delightfully sordid," she said. She was tired but wouldn't dare say it. Claiming tired before two was a sure sign of getting old. "The rain's let up." She stepped toward the lot. "Thanks for the steak and the wine, Mike. We'll have to do this again sometime."

"You good to drive?"

"Sure." But as she walked out, her high heels slipped a bit on the wet pavement. She felt him beside her, yet just behind her as if he'd catch her if she fell. She couldn't decide if the gesture were rude or chivalrous. It was so difficult to know what was what these days.

At her car, she felt in her purse for her keys, and looked up at him studying her as if he were measuring something.

She stood still, wondered what kind of kiss a man who knocks down walls for a living would give. A jack hammer? A wrecking ball? Or would it be a slow and steady, tearing down thin walls board by board. Her mathematician husband had been tentative, as if calculating just where and how long lips and tongue should move. Her geologist had gone at her full-force, but precise and intense the way a rock climber guesses the danger as he gauges each grip for purchase, but he was always too in a hurry to get to the peak. She couldn't remember why she was so quick to find love and then so eager to bolt, leave anything like love behind. Her last one had said, you're going to be a lonely old woman, Hope. No kids, no family, no man. Just a lonely old woman. She'd smacked him in the face for that.

Mike stroked the back of her head, said, "Sweetie, you're too buzzed to go."

"I was just thinking," she said.

"You were dreaming on your feet, professor." He held her hand, squeezed it. She liked the strength of his palm.

Ok, she thought, he's going to kiss me now. He lifted her hand to his mouth and gave a light brush with his lips.

She liked the feel of his beard on her skin, the moist pressure of his lips.

He moved beside her, leaned against her car, not seeming to mind the wetness there. He lifted his face up, closed his eyes, breathed. Then he looked at her as if this were just the beginning of the evening and not the end. "Smell it," he said. "I love that smell of rain on pavement."

She breathed the acrid scent still in the air. "It should smell cleaner by now with all that rain. But it still smells like a parking lot."

"That's 'cause it is a parking lot."

"Back home," she said. "When it rains you smell the dirt and the water and the trees. It's like you know you're an animal when you're out in it. You smell. . . " She searched for the word.

He leaned, whispered, breath warm on her neck. "Fecundity of earth."

She laughed. "Where'd you learn to talk like that?"

He shrugged. "I watch PBS sometimes. I know a lot more than you think I know, professor. I know one way to get in a woman's pants is to get her laughing."

"Oh," she said. "Is that what you're after?"

"That's what I'm after." He put his hands in his pockets, and looked up as if something might happen in that sodden sky.

She looked down, saw her red pedicured nails and strappy black sandals. Her legs were still lean, long under the short skirt. She'd dressed for a man to pick her up, throw her down and screw her. She figured she had about a decade left to dress like this. Still, she was grateful for the soft light of the restaurant, and now the darkness. If she were to sleep with him, in the light of morning he would see the lines at her eyes and lips, the age creeping across the back of her hands, sags slipping at her throat. And those tiny spiderweb creases growing between her breasts. But then, he'd said he liked all kinds of woman: heavy, skinny, young, not so young. He'd named every kind of woman as something he'd be after. He just loved the chase, he'd said. But he'd never mentioned the pleasure of chasing someone old. No one, not even he, wanted old.

He gave her a glance. "You all right?"

"Yeah, I was just thinking."

"You do too much thinking."

"I was thinking you're something of a swashbuckler when it comes to things like...." She was thinking of sex, but said, "Romance."

He laughed. "Swashbuckler. I like that. So pirate, wild,

and bad. But Johnny Depp never got laid in that movie, wasn't even interested. I'm no pirate. But I am the kind of man should be wearing a sign: Beware all you ladies. This is the devil here."

"Don't flatter yourself. You're not a devil, you're just a dog." She had the urge to yawn, swallowed it back, and felt the little surge of moisture in her eyes. "It's time to get on home." She beeped the car unlocked and reached for the door.

"No," he said. He grabbed her, his mouth covering hers. One hand squeezed at the back of her neck; his other hand squeezed her ass. I'm too old for this, she thought, but she let him at her. It had been months, almost a year since she'd been touched by a man. He pressed her against the cold dampness of her car and pulled her into him. His hand was warm under her shirt, squeezing her back, fingers running along her bra strap, then reaching to find the clasp in front, unhooking it. His hand was warm, soft and firm on her breast as if he really, really appreciated what he was holding there. The other hand squeezed between her legs, not poking past the panties like some eager boy, just a gentle pressure, a slight stroking and releasing as if coaxing a stunned animal to move. He pulled her skirt up around her hips, lifted her to the hood of her car.

She thought, stop, but couldn't say it.

"Look at you," he whispered. She looked down, saw her thighs spread taut and smooth and this man moving between them. This is like one of those steamy scenes, she thought, animal man tearing at French lingerie, a perfect moment in soft core porn. But such a cliché. He lifted her quick and yanked her panties to her thighs, his fingers pushed in. She grabbed his wrist. "Stop. You have to stop now."

He straightened. "Why?"

"I'm not ready," she said.

He pulled back, rubbed his fingers together, grinned. "Yes, you are."

"People get arrested for things like this."

"Not me," he said. "Keith, the guard, he'd just laugh."

She looked toward the Taco Bell where Keith was busy with his flexible girlfriend in a truck.

"I know this place," he said. "We might as well be on the dark side of the moon."

She looked out at the parking lot spreading dark and wet around them.

"Keith won't come back until he sees my truck is gone. Anybody driving by, all they gonna see is that goddamned boat at the edge of the lot, because that's the only bit of light around."

I'm a professor, she thought, half naked with a man in a parking lot. She looked at him, his shirt open, his thick muscled chest. She wanted it. He stood there, cool, patient, just waiting for her to give in. She smiled, shook her head and said, "We're a long way from Derbyshire."

"What?"

"It's a place. In a book. A place where people don't do things like this."

"Well sweetie, this is the world where people do things exactly like this." He grazed his palm across her breast, a gentle movement, just enough to make her nipple rise.

"This is ridiculous," she said. She looked down at herself, white breasts, flat belly, long thighs. "If this were a movie, it'd be pretty hot."

"It *is* pretty hot." He took her nipple with his mouth and sucked while her body grew small under the weight of him, and she gave and gave until all she felt was a fluttering whir. She could feel him pulling at her panties, felt them snag at the back of her knee. He pulled until she felt the silk slip off her ankles. He tossed them and went for his zipper.

She slid off the hood pulled down her skirt. "No," she said. "Not here. Not like this." She tried to see in the darkness around her, wondered where her panties went. She stood, buttoning her shirt. "We can't do this yet. You don't even know who I am."

He stepped back and studied her, as if she were a blurry thing on the horizon just coming into focus. "Yes I do. You are a woman named Hope in the dark." He grinned. "How's that for a metaphor?"

"Too obvious," she said. She crouched and looked around on the pavement. "Where are my panties?"

"Maybe I ate them," he said.

"It's good stuff. French silk."

"Okay, Miss French Silk. I guess you're not a first-date-do-it-kind of gal," he said.

"I'm not," she said. And she wasn't, not really, just sometimes.

"We'll find your panties," he said. "Just so you know I can be a gentleman when I have to." He opened his truck, fumbled in the glove-box. He pulled out a flashlight, clicked it, re-clicked, no light. "Dead," he said. Sometimes my son plays with it."

He tossed it back inside. "We'll use my lighter." He flicked on the flame and they bent to search the pavement. "Here's your purse," he said.

She took it, held it to her chest, didn't want to admit she'd forgotten all about her purse.

"And your keys," he said. "Now on to the panties." He gave her a grin. "It's like a treasure hunt." They crouched together and looked.

"Jesus," she said. "I knew you tossed them, but how far can a pair of panties go?'

"All the way to heaven if they're French."

She laughed, and then the rain came pounding down.

They stood up, laughing, drenched. "My poor panties," she said.

"Your poor hair." He pushed the mess of it back from her face. "Let's wait in my truck until it stops." She let him open the door, climbed in, watched him walk around the front and get in his side. He handed her a roll of paper towels from the back seat and she mopped at her face knowing her mascara had run, her foundation had smeared to reveal the blotchy, aging, everyday woman she was. She wished for lipstick, a mirror, a light, for two minutes alone to repair the damage of being smudged, smeared and rained on. She had wanted to think that when she walked away tonight, it would be with some kind of grace. She could smell his cologne still, the scent of cigar in his shirt, but more than anything she smelled the wet sweat smell of her hair. "Do I smell like a dog?" she said.

"A dog?"

"A black friend of mine once said when a white woman's hair got wet, it smelled like a dog. She said there was nothing worse than getting stuck in an elevator with a bunch of white women who'd just been caught out in the rain."

"You smell like a woman," he said. "I wish you'd let me fuck you. We both could use the stress relief."

"Yeah," she said. "We could."

"But I'm not the kind to fight you for it."

"So the prince of darkness *is* a gentleman."

"Yeah," he said. "I am." He wiped his face dry and looked out at the boat glimmering in the flickering light and rain. "God, I love that boat."

"You thinking of buying it?"

"I have a boat. We had some great times on that boat. My wife, she'd sunbathe naked out in the middle of the lake. I taught my son to fish. Good times. Until I started screwing around. But that's another story."

"There's always another story," she said. God she hoped he wasn't going into how his marriage went wrong. "Let's have no sad stories. It's too late for sad stories." She reached in her purse for her compact, dabbed some powder on.

"Yeah," he said. "But you should see my boat. It's a 1967 Owens. Twin engines. Turns on a dime. Got two bedrooms, two baths, perfect wood, all mahogany and teak. Old brass fixtures. A true beauty, and I got it for change. Some guy's wife died of breast cancer, then he kind of went nuts on coke and booze and women. Lost his job. Was selling off everything he had. Living the life, I guess to make up for the grief. Two days after I bought that boat he died. Crashed in the brand new red Mercedes, he'd bought with her insurance money. Wasn't much left for their kid."

While he talked she'd managed to quick fix some lipstick on and give some kind of shape to her hair. "That's awful," she said.

"Damn good timing on my part. Got a hell of a boat." His gaze remained on the boat out there in the dark. He glanced at her, looked away. "It's not like anything was my fault."

"No," she said. "He did it himself."

"We all do it ourselves."

"I dated a guy once, he said with a hundred bucks and a boat you could get just about any woman you want."

Mike made a huffing sound, something like a laugh, but not. "For a night." He poked her in the arm as if they were old buddies. "How long did he have you?"

"Two or three times I think. I never even got the boat ride. It was winter. Guess I lost interest by spring."

"You lost interest by two or three times." He sighed, leaned back in his seat. "Guess I'm shit out of luck, 'cause my boat's in storage now, has been for years. And to tell you the truth I'm in debt to my ass, and don't have the cash to pay the storage fees, so it sits in dry dock, the fees just rising. I know I'm gonna have to face it, let it go. Some things float and some things, you gotta let 'em sink."

She nodded, thinking about sex, thinking about whether they'd have another go at trying to do it or if they'd already decided to let it go. She remembered the hundred-bucks-and-a-boat man. He moved fast. Just went at her the way Mike did. She remembered he had a little penis, but was really good with his hands. She knew Mike didn't have a little penis. She'd felt enough of him to know he'd feel good inside. She knew he'd feel even better holding her afterward, rubbing on her back, burying her in the thick weight of his arms. No matter how the sex went she always loved the feeling of being held when it was over, that sense of comfort, ease, even when the guys were pretty much strangers, there was this little moment of peace after the surge of blood and sweat and saliva and cum had done what it does in the end. But this man had just had his fingers inside her, had grinned, rubbing his fingers together, and said, *You're ready.*

And she had said no. And now she was waiting for the rain to ease so she could climb in her car, all damp and chilled to go home, where there was nothing but a stack of papers to grade and books, so many books, piled, half-read by her bed.

"But there's always more boats," he said. He looked at her. "The rain's eased up. You want to have another look for those panties?"

She looked at his face, the mouth that made her feel like a thing sweetly swallowed, consumed. "Nope," she said. "I want you." She climbed to his side of the truck and straddled him.

"There you go," he said squeezing her hip with one hand and reaching beneath the seat with the other. She heard the hum of the machinery as the seat moved back, giving room. She rose up, unbuttoned her blouse, unhooking her bra, hoping he'd put his mouth on her again.

He unzipped his pants, bucked up a little to yank them past his knees. She could smell this sex, a scent like simmering onions and meat. He took her face with one hand, grinned at her. "Look out, you're running with the dogs, now."

She wished she could say something smart, something witty, something he might remember. But he pulled her to him, shoved his tongue in her mouth and squeezed at her nipple until it hurt. She pulled back.

He grabbed her hips, lifted her a little, then settled her onto him the way he might have set a beam in place. He closed his eyes, and she smiled at the little gasp he gave, the sound men make when a woman opens, lets a man push in. He held her there. "Not too fast," he whispered.

Then they went at it, without a word. She remembered her panties out there on the pavement, remembered a line of soft porn she'd read as a teenager. At her boarding school, there were no greater pleasures than good chocolate sent from mothers and soft porn stolen from big sisters. They'd read it together, savoring the good parts and laughing at blur of soft breasts heaving, and quivering members thrusting, and all the usual things that made sex on a page. But the line she precisely remembered was about a girl being pressed against a tree by the boy she wanted, and how she "stamped her steaming panties to the ground." At fourteen and a virgin, she knew she wanted one day to be that girl, being pushed by some guy who wanted it and she'd give it stamping her steaming panties to the ground.

He gave a thrust, and she pushed back. Eyes shut, rain

pounding all around, they humped faster, nothing elaborate, just a hanging on and going at it. She came hard and fast, heard his little laugh. "Damn what was that? Ten seconds?"

She nodded, kept moving, her eyes closed. "Come on," she said, hoping he'd come soon, that he wouldn't soften and they'd have to get started all over. Men his age, could come quick or rise and soften and take all night long to get off. He grabbed her hips, pulled her up and down, going hard, whispering, "Shit, shit, shit this is good." Then silence. Then the air shuddered with his deep groaning. She'd forgotten the sound a big man can make when he comes, like a roar of a mountain falling down.

She leaned into him, nuzzled her face against his neck, felt his heart against her chest. He patted her back the way teammates do, kissed the top of her head, then lifted her off him. She climbed over to her side, pulled her skirt down and wondered how rude it would be to just grab her purse, get out, and go home. He took her hand then, squeezed with a gesture that would be something like affection, but she knew it was just his way of being polite. So she settled back into the plush sheep skin cover of the seat, closed her eyes and listened to the rain pounding harder now. The truck seemed to rock with the storm. She opened her eyes, ran her fingers through the sheepskin seat cover and gripped it as if she needed to hang on. "Listen to that rain."

"It's coming down." He yanked up his pants, zipping then leaning back in his seat. He closed his eyes. "I needed that." He sighed and settled deeper in his seat. He rubbed his palm up and down her forearm, patted the back of her hand, then leaned back in his seat and closed his eyes. "This is nice," he said.

"Yeah," she said. She sat there wondering how long she should wait. His breath was already deepening in the sound men make when committed to sleep. Five breaths and he'd be out. She counted. Yep, he was gone. She wondered how long she should wait for the rain to let up, while his wetness grew sticky between her legs. Soon she would need to pee. She rubbed a clear space in the window, looked out to the darkness, the empty lot, the boat out there rocking in the gusting wind as if it could break free from its moorings, drift off.

He made a little snoring sound, jerked. She hoped he was awake, but he settled back to sleep as if he were safe, secure, stretched out at home. She wished she could let go like that, go unconscious by simply closing her eyes, flicking a switch. "You are a good animal," she said. He didn't seem to hear her. Animals didn't need bottles of wine, aroma therapy, Ambien, to go to sleep. They just got comfortable, sank down, closed their eyes, clicked off, then with another click could spring awake fully aware of what comfort or threat was around.

His breath stayed deep and steady. She sighed, hooked her bra, buttoned her shirt and wondered again about her panties. They were lost. She looked out at the parking lot shimmering like a shallow lake on the rise. She imagined her silk panties swirling in some puddle, lifting with the flow of pools forming, eddying down toward the drain in the dark. By morning they're be somewhere in the sewage drain in the mix of Taco Bell bags and cigarette butts, the remains of things enjoyed, and dropped, tossed, let go. That was the way of things of this world. Except love, she thought. But no, love like anything else wore out, expired in time, got tossed.

He made a grumbling sound, shifted a bit in his seat toward his window like a man who was accustomed to sleeping in cars. She wished he had held her a little longer, just a little. So went the disadvantage of screwing in cars or trucks or even upscale SUV's with aftermarket ultra-plush seats.

She lay back and listened to the rhythm of his breath. It was late, but it would be a long, long while until the grey light of morning. She looked at the Commander out there, brave, as if ready for any ride the storm could offer. She didn't know anyone who could afford a boat like that. She leaned back, looked at it through half-closed eyes. It seemed to rock on water, a gentle rhythmic movement. "It's like it's moving," she said, but she knew the illusion of moving was just the effect of her breath rising, falling. Nothing was really going anywhere.

Mike made a little grunting sound, stirred, then as if by choice sank back to the deep breath of sleep. She reached and took his hand, wanting to feel something of the man who'd just been inside her. She squeezed his hand, got no response. He was gone. She let go, sat back in her seat and closed her eyes. She remembered a poem, the first she'd ever remembered by rote. She spoke it softly with the cadence it needed, something like a song, but not. "Oh western wind where wilt thou blow, the small rain down can rain."

He stirred up, gave her a wide awake and friendly look. "I like that," he said. "The small rain down can rain."

"How long have you been awake?"

"In and out," he said. "Then I heard that. It was like you were telling me something."

"It's just a poem that came to mind. Want to hear the rest?"

He cleared his throat, reached under his seat for a bottle of water. "Not really, but I bet I'm gonna hear it." He took a swig and offered it to her. "I'm not sure how fresh it is, but you want a sip?"

She shook her head. "It's only one more line to it. You can handle that."

"Shoot," he said and took another hit of water.

She looked straight ahead, spoke to the Commander as if it were her audience. "Oh Christ, if my love were in my arms and I in my bed again."

He looked at her. "You a Christian?"

"No, I'm not a Christian."

"Good," he said. "I'd feel weird about that."

"It's just a poem," she said.

He held the bottle toward her. "You sure you don't want some of this before I finish it. Screwing makes me thirsty."

She shook her head and watched him gulp down the water. "It's a poem about love, well, about longing I guess. It's anonymous," she said.

"I can't believe you're not thirsty after all that wine. Must be a hundred poems about wine, right."

"Yeah," she said. Oh God. She'd just screwed an idiot.

He was looking at her. "Know any poems about wine?"

"I'm not like a jukebox, plug a quarter in, pick a poem."

"Yeah, I get it. You always so serious?"

"No," she said, thinking yes, wondering when she started believing things were supposed to mean things and got pissed when they didn't.

He reached between the seats, found his keys, and turned on the engine. "We could use a little defrost in here."

She watched as the air hit the windshield, the clarity spreading slowly, steadily from the bottom, rising up to give a clear view of the lot. The rain had stopped and now the boat shimmered as if newly made. All clean.

"Time to get home," she said. She felt around the floorboards for her shoes.

He nodded, stared ahead, hands on the steering wheel, like a taxi driver done with his fare. "Nice time," he said.

Shoes, purse, keys in hand, she opened the door and stepped out. She liked the feeling of her bare feet spread cool and solid on the pavement.

He buzzed the passenger window down, called, "I'll make sure you get started all right."

"I'll be fine." She opened her door, tossed her things inside, but just stood there, looked up at the dark. "It's nice out here," she said. "Cool and fresh, but it still smells like a parking lot."

"That's because—"

"I know," she said. "I know where I am. Go on." She waved him away and made a move to get into her car. He shrugged, gave a little lift of his hand off the steering wheel, then took off. His truck moved across the lot, thick wheels making a whooshing sound that faded as he neared the exit. She watched until she saw him pull out onto the street, disappear into the dark. If this were a story, she thought, that would mean something. She got in her car and started the engine. She liked the feel of her bare feet on the pedals, remembered the way she liked to drive barefoot in high school. She shifted the car into drive, but kept her foot on the brake, tried to make some sense of what she'd just done. But it wasn't a story. No plot, no protagonist, no resolution. It was just another man gone, and a woman going. No meaning at all. But it had to mean something surely. Things had to mean something. Tomorrow, she thought, maybe tomorrow she'd figure it out. She lifted her foot off the brake and let the car rev forward a little on its own. She saw the guard's truck heading her way, just the way Mike said he would. She stomped the gas and moved on.

Are
We
Lucky Yet?

I wanted it to be nice. Me with three kids, and I'd never had a man take me out for Mother's Day. And there was Jerry—not even their dad—telling me he couldn't believe I'd never been out for a Mother's Day dinner, said to me what kind of man you been letting father those kids? I didn't need to tell him because he knew me having kids had nothing to do with having something like a father around.

We met at the court-ordered AA meeting, and you don't want to look down the path a person comes from when it leads to some damp basement of a church where strangers sit in a circle to hear everybody tell the story of their own personal screw-ups. It stinks of sweat and cigarettes and coffee, and it seems like no amount of cleaning can get rid of that smell of people hitting bottom and trying to scratch their way out. It's not the kind of place anyone wants to go, and it's sure as hell is not a place where you go looking for romance with all those horny men jonesing for a drink, and their eyes moving over you with that dull kind of glow that just makes me think of flashlights with the batteries going dead. But Jerry was different. He just gave me a nod when I did that I'm Vickie and I'm an alcoholic thing. I hate saying that. It's like saying that's all you are: a drunk. And everybody's a whole lot more than one thing. But Jerry didn't run his eyes over my boobs and my ass like I was a hot steak on a plate. Just that nod, and for the rest of the meeting he looked at the scars on his hands like he was regretting every drink, every punch, every fight that took him to jail and landed him in a church basement where nobody has a story you want to hear. But Jerry's story took me because he was an only child with a momma who lived in the bottom of a bottle of booze. I could see at first glance he was strong, tattooed muscled arms, and even his back. I could see the muscles through the thin cloth of his shirt. He was good-looking all right, with that dark skin and green eyes, but I liked the way he seemed not to know what he had.

So I had my eye on him, and one day at a meeting he mentioned how it was lonesome to be an only child. I don't remember why he said it, but he said it like it was the beginning of his trouble: it was lonesome to be an only child. I knew I wanted him then, not like a woman just wanting a man between her legs, but more like wanting to hold someone that you can see wants something like love. Well, not really love, because that's too much to ask, but something close to it. And I guess he saw the same thing in me. So one date, and he moved in. I know that breaks the rules, but sometimes you've got to make your own rules.

So it was Mother's Day, our first real holiday since we got together right after New Year's and neither one of us had had a birthday yet. We'd been sober five months, and that should be long enough to be over the dry drunk stage. But we were working at our steps, kept getting stuck on step four and the fearless moral inventory part—that's a place where the lies come so easy, you really can't see the truth of things. But we were pretty good at step one, knowing we were powerless over the booze—well maybe not knowing it, just admitting it in a vague kind of way. I was looking forward to a nice meal where I didn't have to cook or do the dishes, and there'd be no temptation for a drink. We thought we'd be safe in a family place on Mother's Day where kids three and under can eat for free, and the mother gets a rose.

Jerry said a woman like me deserved at least a rose. He's sweet that way. But most don't see that. They just see a muscled-up Mexican-looking guy—even though his mother's Irish. They see the black hair, dark skin, arms covered in tattoos, and they look at him like he's some kind of thug and probably illegal. But if anybody bothered to look at the gentle in his eyes—he has these green, green eyes, all deep and flickering with light. It's like you're looking in a cool spring forest when you're looking into Jerry's eyes. If anybody looked there, they might see the safest place in the world in Jerry. Or maybe if anybody dared to ever ask him a question, they might find out that Jerry is a sentimental kind of man: those tattoos are all reminders of the dead people he's known. They're mostly friends, like the guy Jeff who drowned swimming to the other side of his boat. Jerry still looks surprised when he tells the story, how they'd all been skiing and were anchored in the middle of the lake. And this Jeff said he needed to cool down, so he dove in to swim around the boat, but he never came up. And there was his friend Frank who ran his Harley under a truck, and nobody knows for sure if it was an accident. And there's a cousin who overdosed. But they're not all tragic stories. He's got a tattoo of his granny over his heart. She raised him because his momma couldn't, and he says she deserves the most special place he could offer. He's loyal like that, but try telling that to the fat bitch who couldn't help but snarl her mouth when she saw us—pink lips stretched over dentures too big and white to look anything like real. I should have known when I first caught sight of that mouth of hers I'd be punching her before the day was done. Maybe if I'd been sober a little longer, I would have known to walk away as soon as I took a look at that fat lady's we-don't-want-your-kind-here face.

Like I was saying, I wanted it to be nice. But the baby woke up early that morning. She was fighting an ear infection. I gave her some Tylenol and put her in front of the TV, so I could doze. That lasted about a minute, so she woke up Jerry, and that wasn't good since he didn't get in until four o'clock in the morning from his job as assistant manager and bouncer at The Liqu-er Box bar. It's a strip joint, and he hates it because his momma was a stripper, and he said he hated knowing he was making his paycheck off the tits and twats of fucked-up girls like his momma. He only talks like that when he's really had enough of something, and I guess he wasn't his best self, working that job. But it was hard to find good pay once they let him go at the Jeep factory when they cut production because everything's going to hell these days.

Jerry's always better when he gets his sleep, so I got the baby quiet and snoozing in the rocky swing she was outgrowing. Then I went and rubbed Jerry's back all soft and gentle the way he likes, and I set the fan going on high in the bedroom to cover up the sound of the TV. So I got him back to sleep, and by then Jessie and Tyler were up and fighting over the last bowl of Lucky Charms. They believed in that Leprechaun, fought over the shamrocks, yellow moons, pink hearts. So I divided up the Lucky Charms, and they each got a share of what they wanted. I had to eat the extra pink heart myself so things would work out even. Then I mixed in some Cheerios, and they actually liked the taste better than plain Lucky Charms.

But it wasn't long they were making a racket with their monster trucks on the kitchen floor, so I sent them out back to play. I knew before long Tyler would get busy looking for a four-leaf clover in the back yard. It was one useful thing I learned from my momma. When she wanted me out of the house, she'd send me to the back yard to find a four-leaf clover. She'd say I couldn't come back in until I found one. So I'd look and look, trying to do what my momma said. I was the youngest with my older brother at school, so it was up to me to find the luck. I never did. After awhile it'd get lonely and hot out there. Sometimes I'd try to fake it, tear two leaves off another clover and push the single leaf up between the other three, so it looked like a four-leaf clover as long as I held the two little stems tight in my hand. I'd holler to Momma that I'd found one and run in the kitchen and give it to her. She'd grab it from me, give it a glance, and throw it in the trash. She'd look at me in this disgusted way she had, say, "You can't fake your luck, Vickie." Sometimes she'd tell me I was born to be unlucky like her, said it was in my blood like the blue eyes and blonde hair she gave me. But still she'd make me go out there and keep looking for luck, and I'd do it. It was better than being smacked in the mouth or locked in a closet. I swore to myself that I'd never be a mother like my mother. I promised myself I'd never smack my kids or lock them in a closet. I wanted to be good. I've always wanted to be good.

And as much as I didn't want to live my momma's life I found myself screwing around too much and reaching for the booze every day the way a drowning man claws at the air. But I've quit all that. And I've never hit my kids or locked them in a closet. But I do know the need to send them outside when I just can't take another sound or sight of them. I know it's survival sometimes, the only sensible thing you can do to keep you from screaming or worse. I send the boys out, but not mean the way my momma did. I make it sound like an adventure, so they don't mind. They're still young enough to get excited over magical things—at least Tyler is. Jessie just wants to win. So if Tyler goes to look for a four-leaf clover, Jessie's right on it, not for the luck but to win. He frowns at the ground, rams his fingers through the green as if he could make a lucky clover jump up and surrender. That's his daddy's blood.

They were trying to behave that day. So while Lacey Dawn was sleeping and the boys busy looking for luck, I got the chance to take a shower and flat-iron my hair. I hate my hair most days, all frizz and curls. With enough setting gel and heat, I can get my hair looking like corn silk—that's one of the first things Jerry said he liked about me, my golden corn silk hair. I didn't tell him it wasn't really gold, and that it was really more like a Brillo pad than silk. He found out in time of course just the way I found out he snored something awful from the time his mother's boyfriend broke his nose. They were too poor to ever get it fixed right. He wakes himself up snoring sometimes, and he remembers why he snores so bad, and that just gets him pissed off at his mother all over again.

I wanted him to be happy that day. So I picked out the short blue-jean skirt he likes me to wear. He likes my legs even though I think they're too white and look old with the spider veins already starting because of poor circulation.

My momma always told me not to smoke, said it'd wreck hell on my skin. But like most girls, I never believed anything my mother said, especially if it involved something I didn't want to know. She was hardly an authority on healthy things—died from a wrecked liver at forty-six. She didn't get to live long enough to see Lacey Dawn. I gave my girl my mother's name because it's one pretty thing about my mother, and the name reminds me of Kentucky where my mother was born. I used to love saying my mother's name to try to hold on to something good about her. She had other pretty things, like her baby soft white skin, blue eyes and shiny hair. When I look at her little girl pictures, I think she looks like an angel, and I wonder how such a soft thing grew to be so hard. And I know it was the booze, and the living her life pissed off about everything and out to blame anything but herself. I've forgiven her for all that.

In meetings I learned my mother was a victim of herself, just the way I can be a victim of myself. And I learned sometimes you have to forgive people for things like that. I decided my momma had a right to have a little girl named for her. She always said there was nothing in this world like the laughter of a little girl, but I don't remember her taking much pleasure in me. Once the boys were born, she liked the boys all right, but she was always too sick or drunk to pay them much attention. When I got pregnant again, I told her I was thinking of an abortion, she said hell no, for me to have that baby. She said that child will be a girl, and she'll be a gift, I promise. For a drunk she had a high and mighty way of talking about things. Drunks do that.

I didn't believe her. But I had the baby, not thinking of a gift. It was just a why-not-one-more kind of thing. I never felt like I was any kind of gift to my mother. I just remember all the times she said, "If it weren't for you kids, I'd blow my head off." And I knew she didn't mean it like we were some big joy giving her reason to stay alive. I knew how she meant it. We were the things keeping her tied to this fucked-up world. And I know the feeling. There's days I know if it weren't for my kids, I'd do whatever it took to get out of this life. Not a gun, the way some do. Pills maybe. Or find a way to swim off to the bottom of a bottle and stay there curled and quiet and still as that tequila worm somebody is always daring somebody to eat.

So I was counting on a nice Mother's Day to make up for the nothing ones, the ones that are just another day of dishes and laundry and mouths to feed. And I felt good that day because the Golden Corral was having their new seafood special with fried shrimp and all kinds of fish, and even crab legs. When Jerry saw the commercial on TV he hollered, "That's where I'm taking you for Mother's Day." And I smiled, hoping it'd really happen, and even if it didn't happen I was pleased that Jerry paid attention to all the little things I like. He knew I could eat my weight in fried shrimp if I got the chance. Jerry says watching me eat is right there next to sex, so I was thinking we'd eat until we could hardly move, then we'd come home and put the kids down for a nap, then we'd go to the bedroom to have our own little celebration.

But the minute we pulled in the parking lot of the Golden Corral, and I saw the line of people circled halfway around the building, I knew we'd be in for a challenge. I should have prayed that serenity thing, but all I could think was, God I hope my children behave. And maybe that was what jinxed things—that's what they say about negative thinking. So before we were out of the car, the boys were fussing over how many monster trucks they could take in, and I said they could have one each, and I told them if they didn't behave I'd throw the damn trucks away. They knew better than that—I can't afford to throw anything away. I just hide their toys sometimes, and later on when they're being really good or maybe a little bit bored, the toys come back out, and I tell them Santa's elves brought them back even though it isn't Christmas. I tell them Santa's elves can do all kinds of magic when little boys behave.

So we headed for the restaurant, and Tyler and Jesse raced across that parking lot to get in line. With them being boys, they didn't know the power of their speed, so when they tried to stop, they crashed into an old man with a cane. They nearly knocked him down, but another man steadied him. I gave him a little wave of thanks, but he just stared at me, and everyone else in the line turned to stare at my boys who were squealing and came running back toward me. Then of course, the whole crowd stared at me: the mom who couldn't handle her kids. I knew what they saw: a skinny blonde welfare witch. I knew they figured Jerry to be a Mexican who couldn't be the daddy to my kids being the boys are red-headed freckled things, and Lacey Dawn is all blonde and blue-eyed like me.

Once the old man got steady, he moved back toward a woman who patted his arm and gave us a look like we were some fast food trash someone had thrown to the pavement. There was a little crowd that gathered around him, then a little bit of laughing as they looked back our way. So I lit a cigarette, just the way they probably expected me to do, and I said, "Come on kids. It's Mother's Day." And we got in place at the back of the line. Jerry was holding the baby— he's better at keeping her calm. I think that thick warm muscled heat of him makes her feel safe. She just held to his shoulder and looked out at the people in line. She likes to watch people. Just take her to the grocery store and it's like taking most kids to a zoo. But the boys, like most boys, they're always after the next thing they can get their hands on to take it apart or throw around. So it wasn't five minutes they were pushing at each other, asking me when they were going to get their ice cream cone. "After dinner," I said, and I pulled out their monster trucks from the diaper bag. Then the boys sat on the sidewalk vrooomming those trucks all around, smashing them into each other and throwing them in the air. Before long I saw some people looking at my boys and laughing at the way they played. There's something about twins. I guess it makes people happy to know sometimes God can do exactly the same thing twice. They think it's cute, some kind of mini-miracle. So I was starting to feel easy about things.

I put my cigarette out in the ashcan to go in. When we were just inside the door, I saw this family turn and stare at us. The man was wearing a sport coat like he'd just left church. His wife was done up in one of those flower-print dresses with a bow at the neck—the kind of thing nobody ought to wear. I saw her nudge her two girls ahead as if my boys might give them lice or something. I told myself to pull back from that kind of thinking. Lacey Dawn started giggling and bouncing in Jerry's arms and pointing at all the people rushing around with plates piled high and all the lines of food laid out and those fake vegetable stands against the wall like the place was some fancy farmer's market. Lacey Dawn always gets excited when she sees something she's never seen, so I guess the Golden Corral was something like Disneyland to her.

At the cashier stand, the girl smiled at me and handed me the rose corsage. She said Happy Mother's Day, and I said thank you, but I couldn't shake the queasy feeling in my gut. I pinned on the corsage myself because Jerry had his hands full with the baby. I stood there and looked out at the restaurant and remembered high school and those cafeteria lines that smelled like grease and salt and steamed bread. I felt a sadness rise up in me, and I didn't know why, but they say when you stop drinking to expect all kinds of feelings to stir up, so I stood there feeling how I hadn't moved so far from those days of taking whatever some old lady in a hair net dumped on my tray.

"Hey," Jerry said. I looked at him. "You're drifting to a bad place, aren't you?" I nodded. He smiled and scratched at the back of my head the way I like. "Why would you drift to a bad place with all these good things right here?" I shrugged and said it was a habit like everything else. Then I smiled at the boys because they were all excited about the NASCAR cups they'd get for their drinks. Jessie kept going on about how they'd get to take the cups home for free. He's his daddy's son all right, always itching to get something for free.

Everybody wants something for nothing, but nobody wants it like the boys' daddy, Perry McNabb. When he first sat at my station at the Cracker Barrel, I knew something more would come from him than a good tip. He was a big handsome man with arms thick as my waist, but I could see that he had careful hands by the way he moved his knife and fork. They were the kind of hands a woman wants on her skin. He gave me this big smile like I was the first blue sky he'd seen after a month of cloudy days. We joked a little every time I went by his table. He said that in spite of my uniform, he could see I had class. He said he could see at first glance that I was more than a fried fish and cornbread kind of girl. I thought that was funny because that's just what he was eating, along with green beans and applesauce. So I said sure when he asked me on a date. He took me to a Japanese steak house where they do all those tricks throwing the food around. He laughed at how good I was when the chef would toss a shrimp, and I could catch it without a smear straight into my mouth.

He said he ran a car lot, and every date he'd take me out

for a ride in a different car: Mustangs, old Cadillacs, even a Corvette a couple of times. He'd drive and smile like he owned everything he drove. I was impressed. I like nice cars and some guy to buy my dinner. We screwed around. And it was lots at the beginning. He gave me a silver chain necklace, real silver, so I thought that meant something even if he did just hand it to me out of his pocket. Then he started showing up less and less, and the sex was just a getting-it-done kind of thing. After awhile he stopped calling, wouldn't take my calls. I went to his car lot looking for him, which is the thing stupid girls do, like thinking if you rub an old lamp long enough a genie will pop out.

But no magic came from Perry McNabb, just babies. At the car lot I met his brother, who really owned the lot. Perry was nothing but a repo man. Those cars he drove all came from his brother's used car lot—he got good deals on the repos—and Perry got to keep whatever was in the car—like leather jackets, CD's, things like that silver necklace I wound up selling at a pawn shop. When I told his brother I was pregnant with Perry's child, he just gave me this pat on the shoulder like he was some old friend and said, "Ah that's too bad, Vickie, what you going to do?"

I pulled back, said, "Me?" I looked him in the eyes, blue and all full of tricks just like Perry.

"I don't know where he is, Vickie," he said. "Last I heard he was working on a deal to dump hazardous waste in Mexico." He shrugged and looked out at the car lot like he was proud. "You know Perry, always looking for a way to make something from nothing." He laughed that coughing sound men do when they've got something shady on their minds. "They got a good thing going down there. US dollars buy places to dump hazardous shit in Mexico. The Mexican mayors collect the cash, and by the time people get sick from living near the shit, nobody can trace just who did what when.

And you know how it is." He gave a little shrug and said, "Nobody really gives a damn about some poor Mexicans getting sick." Then he looked down at my belly, up to my boobs, then my face. "Too bad for you, little chica."

I slapped him, but he just took my wrist and smiled. "You'll never find my brother. He's like one of those hyenas, they just eat what they want and blend back in with all those other hyenas hiding in the hills."

Just my luck to have twins by that man.

We finally got our trays and ordered our drinks. And I was feeling good because the boys passed for three without a question from the cashier, so they were getting to eat free. It's the little breaks you've gotta be grateful for because the big ones are so long in coming. It was all going smooth with nobody asking anything until the fat bald manager walked by, and Jessie dropped his monster truck on the floor. The fat man huffed and puffed as he bent to pick up the truck and give it to Jessie, said, "That's a mighty big truck for a little boy. How old are you?" And of course Jessie puffed up and said, "I'm not a little boy. I'm four going on five. I'm big." There was this freeze in the air as the manager looked at the receipt coming up on the register. He looked it over and shoved it at the cashier who gave me a sad "I tried" look. I just shrugged. "Charge for those kids," the manager said and gave us one of those disgusted looks before he walked away. I could feel the eyes of the people behind us. One woman said it, just loud enough, "Imagine trying to steal from the Golden Corral when they're giving away roses on Mother's Day." I gave her my fuck-you-bitch glare, and I looked to Jerry who was busy getting more money from his pocket and holding Lacey Dawn.

So I took her from him, and she wailed and kicked her feet like a baby when she was almost two and big enough to know better. I jiggled and shushed her. I watched Jerry bend to the waitress and point out the table where he'd like to sit across the room. And I went to follow her, happy for someone else to be carrying trays for me for a change. Then I saw the boys heading for the fried chicken piled high under a heat lamp. I yelled "Stop it right there," and the whole restaurant looked my way. I just snuggled up Lacey Dawn. The smell of her calms me, and I followed the waitress who'd already put a basket of bread and plates on the table. I gave Lacey Dawn a roll to chew on and watched the boys coming back with their hands full of chicken legs. They sat tearing at the chicken and swinging their legs like the party was just getting started. "Boys," I said, "You need to listen. There's a way of doing things in a restaurant." Then I heard a lady next to us say, "This isn't a zoo!"

I looked up and saw her. The pig bitch with this snarly look on her face. And there across from her was this older skinny woman who must have been her mother because she was wearing a rose. She gave me a glare and went to stabbing at the food on her plate. But the pig bitch—and I swear she looked like a pig in her too tight pink pantsuit— she said, "You could try training those kids. This isn't a zoo." I looked at the cheap big gold cross dangling on her giant boobs, like she had to yell out that she was a Christian for any one to know. You sure couldn't tell it from her ways. I wanted to say fuck off, bitch, but the waitress showed up with the drinks. Tyler reached and, of course, knocked his drink into the breadbasket, and Coke was running everywhere. I saw those bitches shaking their heads. I yelled, "Tyler, I told you there's a way of doing things. Now sit back while I get this cleaned up." I looked around for Jerry.

I could feel the fat pig lady still staring at the mess on my table, enjoying it, her eyes all squinty. She looked at the old woman with no chin who looked all grey and leathery and wrinkled as a lizard, and she said, "Some little brats should never be let out of the house." The old woman put her lips tight, gave a little shake of her head, and bent back to stabbing at her green beans.

Jerry was suddenly there with towels he got from a waitress, and he started sopping up the mess. I asked if we could find another table. I couldn't imagine eating a nice meal with these women glaring at me, but the waitress was helping him, and the mess was clean, and she gave him that smile all women do. Then she remembered to smile at me before she walked away.

I could see the strain in Jerry's jaw, hear that exhale thing he does, a long slow blowing breath they taught him to do in an anger management class. He patted my hand, said, "Come on, Vickie. This is your day. I know how you like to sit next to a window." And then I saw we were next to a window. He must've scouted out the only six-top table next to a window and told the waitress to lead us to it. He looked around the room and said, "Besides it's not like there's a lot of moving room." He sat and sipped his Mountain Dew, and I saw the pig bitch glaring at the ink on his arms. Then she gave me a look like I was the sour dishrag left on the counter.

Then I saw her looking at my bare legs and my short skirt, and I wiggled to pull my skirt a little lower on my legs and that bumped the baby in the table, and she hollered like I'd pinched her, and before she could get really going, Jerry plopped a piece of ice on the table and flicked it at her. She watched it spin and grabbed for it and laughed. Then Jerry leaned to me and said "Shhh," like I was the baby about to scream. "Happy Mother's Day," he said. And I felt good because I pretty much always feel good when I'm looking at Jerry. Then the waitress brought the high chair. And I kissed Lacey Dawn's head and said, "Look here, baby."

Most times she's good about sitting in a high chair because I tease her and call her a little queen sitting on her throne, but her high chair at home is all pink and glittery. I painted it that way special for her, and the one at the restaurant was just that chipped and dirty brown thing you see everywhere. She didn't want anything to do with that chair. She clung to me and pulled at my shirt like I was trying to throw her into a fire. So I gave up and held her and she looked at me like she'd won the fight, and she had. It pisses me off sometimes the way a kid, not even two, gets all proud over any little win. I was ready to tie her down in the high chair, and then Jerry got her busy watching him pour lemonade into her sippy cup. And I thought what-the-fuck, a man, a frigging bouncer at a titty bar was better at mothering my babies than me. I mean I'm grateful, but sometimes his goodness just seems too good, and I start wondering if he sneaks a drink now and then to keep the calm he has, and I get pissed.

I wanted a drink. I was aching for a shot of vodka, just a little bit of numb. I wanted a drink so bad, my head was stinging and tears were burning at my eyes. I sipped my Mountain Dew and the cold and the sweetness did help. I eased back then, smiled at Jerry. I wanted to tell him I loved him, but with the pig bitch and the lizard lady watching every move we made, I didn't want to share any kind of tender thing they might tear at. So I just looked at him and gave him what I could of a smile. Sometimes I think if I had said it, if I had put that little bit of love out there in that big noisy room where everybody was just set on gorging themselves for cheap, maybe if I had put something soft and true out there in room, the day would have changed. But my mother didn't raise a soft girl. She raised a hard girl, so I glared back at the pig lady, and shifted in my seat just to make my skirt rise a little higher on my thigh.

Jerry said he'd take the boys to get their food and he'd bring back macaroni and a treat for the baby. He said when he got back I could go at that seafood bar and take my time to get anything I wanted. Then he smiled, and I felt like crying he was so nice to me.

I watched the people out there, eating their food, little girls done up with curls and their little croc shoes decorated with bows and butterflies. And I looked down at my Lacey Dawn who smelled like a mix of baby shampoo and little sweaty curls, and I was happy for a second because there is something about your baby's sweat that's sweet and yours, and makes you feel you've done something right in the world. So I kept breathing the smell of her hair and kept thinking if I could keep my mind on her sweetness, I wouldn't have to think about the bitches at the next table.

At meetings, they teach you how bad thoughts lead to feelings and certain feelings lead to a drink. And I was fighting those thoughts, thoughts like every thing in the world is ugly and mean so why not just get numb to it, and drink. So I sat there trying to think of things to make me like the world, things like Jerry and my boys when they're behaving, and Lacey Dawn.

Then I saw them, a group of Christians all standing around a table just across the room. They held hands and bent their heads to pray over their food. They were the old-time Church of God I figured: the women with their dresses below the knees and their long-to-the-waist hair, and the men all in dark pants and starched button down shirts. There was a preacher who was stood taller than the rest and led the prayer. I couldn't hear the words, just a faint deep murmuring. It was a peaceful sound, and it seemed the whole place got a little more quiet, a little more still to show respect, or some of them just to gawk, I guess. They had a peace all around them that you had to notice. They had God. I could almost see the Holy Spirit, like a warm light hovering over their heads, keeping them peaceful and grateful and safe. The prayer ended and they each gave each other's hand a little shake and sat to eat, not in a hungry way, but something more at ease, at peace. I watched them, wishing I could be sitting at their table, wishing I could be in that family of faith. But I'd tried that, failed. I remembered my preacher, the last man who ever laid a hand on me with a prayer.

His name was Luke—at least that's what he called himself. I met him at a church—which is where drunks sometimes go for help, and then when it fails, in time they wind up in some other church basement with a bunch of drunks. He was a powerful preacher—they said he'd had the calling since he was thirteen, and I suppose he did with that voice so strong and smooth. They called him Brother Luke. Even I called him Brother Luke—whispered Brother Luke when he kissed my neck and unbuttoned my shirt, then breathed his name in little gasping sounds when he pushed between my legs that day in the woods by the stream. He pushed, and I pushed with him, and we pushed and panted like wild things on that quilt until we came and both fell back laughing.

The first time he ever laid his hands on my head to pray for my soul, I knew it wouldn't be long before he'd be in my clothes. He had these fingers that when they moved through your hair to hold your head, you could feel the strength of them moving down your neck to your chest and your belly to that quivering place between your legs. When he suggested we meet in the woods by the creek so we could pray and let him baptize me, I knew what was coming. I left the boys with my momma who always just shrugged and lit a cigarette when I said I was going to the church. I let him take me to the place far back in the mountains, and we knelt on the quilt with the Bible between us. I let him pray not hearing his words, just feeling his hands move over my head while he whispered hard and fast it was like a soft pleading, and I felt the pleading inside me not for God, but for Luke's hands to slip inside my clothes. Brother Luke never gave me the gift of the Holy Spirit, but he did give me another kind of spirit. Her name's Lacey Dawn, and I guess there are times when she feels something like religion, gives me a kind of peace.

I was thinking about Luke's hands when I saw Jerry and the boys coming back. I felt guilty, like the dirty tramp those women thought I was, sitting there thinking about sex with another man while Jerry was looking after my kids. The boys' plates were piled with chicken and okra, macaroni and corn. Jerry slid next to me and held a piece of shrimp to my mouth. Lacey Dawn reached to grab it, but I opened my mouth quick, let Jerry pop it in my mouth. And Lacey Dawn did what we all want to do when something we want goes poof. She screamed, kicked her feet and flailed like somebody had just poked her with a hot iron. Jerry tried to give her another piece of shrimp from his plate, but that set her to squirming trying to get off my lap where she could roll around the floor. There was nothing to do but let her wear herself out because the more you try to stop her, the more fight she puts in it. The boys just kept eating and laughing at her. But pig lady turned in her chair, and I could see this big hairy mole on her chin. She looked straight at me, and said, "That brat acts like an animal." I couldn't argue—she was acting wild. But I just looked dead on at the bitch and said, "My child is not your business." She turned back to her plate and said to the old woman, loud enough for me to hear, "Trailer trash." And I got so mad I could hear that buzzing sound in my head.

Then I saw Jerry lean to Lacey Dawn, and say all soft and calm and teasing, "I've got some chocolate ice cream on a spoon." She went silent, looked up at him as if she didn't quite trust him, then he reached, and I saw the little bowl he'd sneaked on his tray. He dug the spoon in, scooped up a bite of ice cream, showed it to Lacey Dawn, and said "You can have it if you'll climb into my lap and be good." And the boys, of course, started shouting, "No fair!" I heard the bitch say, "Monsters," and I got that metal feeling in my stomach, and I gave a look to Jerry, and he knew what I was feeling. I'd told him about the time I smacked a bitch with a napkin dispenser in a bar. He gave me a nod like it would be all right, told me to go on and get my dinner, that he'd take care of the baby and the boys.

I got up, looked at the old woman grab a fork of potatoes and poke it in her mouth. I'd never seen such ugly eating, the two of them there, just shoving it in. "This your daughter?" I said to the old one. She just moved those potatoes around in her mouth the way old people do and glared at me. "You must have worked hard to raise such a big fat bitch." The old lady's eyes just popped, and the pig bitch made a move like she'd hit me. I was ready.

But Jerry was up and between us. "She's sorry," Jerry said. I looked around. People were staring. The Christians were taking little quick looks my way. "No, I'm not sorry," I said. "Now I think I'll get something to eat." I felt them all looking at me. Even the boys and Lacey Dawn had gone still. I wasn't hungry. But I went for that seafood counter, hell bent on getting my money's worth whether I ate it or not.

When I got back to our table, I saw the waitress standing there asking the bitches if they'd like to move to another part of the restaurant. The pig bitch gave me a glance with those squinty eyes, shook her head, her jowls trembling. "No," she said. "We were here first. We've got every right to sit at this table and finish our meal." I saw her reach across the table, grab a plate piled high with sweet potato-marshmallow casserole and scoop some on her plate. Then she scooped some to her momma's plate, and I could hear the plopping sound.

I'd given up on being hungry. But I sat, and I thought if I could just break open one crab leg, dip the meat in butter sauce I'd be in a better mood. Then Jessie, being Jessie, had to grab a crab leg and go at Lacey Dawn, saying something like the crab monster was gonna bite her. And of course that got her to screaming. She lunged out of Jerry's lap, and slid across my legs to the floor. I knew she was going to go running, so I reached to grab her arm, but she pulled free and fell back into the thigh of the pig lady who jumped back and swung her arm and knocked Lacey Dawn to the floor. All I know next was the smack of my fist on her jaw.

I don't remember getting up to do it, just the smack of my fist. She put her hand on her face, stared up at me. Then she wobbled her jaw a little, reached in that hole of a mouth of hers and pulled out the denture. I guess I knocked it lose, so she went to trying to put it back in, and dropped it on the floor. And I guess I couldn't help but laugh a little, so she stood and took a swing at me. But I'm good at dodging, and with her being so fat she lost her balance and fell into our table, her arms flailing. She knocked Tyler in the mouth, and he sat there, eyes staring up and making this gasping sound. It seemed like everybody was screaming. And I was ready to knock the bitch down, but Jerry grabbed my arm, slammed me to the chair. When he turned, she was coming at him with a butter knife, and he did some karate move he knows, knocked the knife loose, twisted her arm back and had her pinned against the wall.

And of course that's when the cops showed, and I know what they saw, some tattooed Mexican pinning some poor old lady against the wall. The cops were all over him. They tazed him, and I saw him drop like a dead man to the ground.

Even the kids sat silent. It was like the whole world stopped. Lacy Dawn started this low little whimpering sound. I tried to reach for Jerry, and that's when the old lizard lady hollered, "She's the one, she started it, she punched my daughter in the face." And the cop looked at me, and the fat bitch hissed, "She looks like a crack whore to me." And before I knew it, one cop's got Lacey Dawn and carrying her off screaming, and the other one's hand-cuffing me and pulling me out the door. I heard the boys wailing, and I looked back, and saw a lady cop leading the boys off and the other one jiggling Lacey Dawn, trying to calm her down. There were other cops were standing over Jerry like he might jump up and go crazy any minute.

"Eyes forward," the cop said to me, and he pushed. But I kept trying to look back to see if anyone was looking kindly on me, to see if anyone saw the way the fat bitch knocked my baby down. I looked toward the Christians who were all standing, but still and close and quiet-looking like a bunch of deer you run across in the woods. I hoped they saw the truth—they're supposed to see the truth in things. I tried to catch the preacher man's eye, but I couldn't see anyone's eyes for the crying in mine, and the knowing it was going to be bad, just when I was getting straight.

So they got me outside, and I saw them emptying my purse out on the hood of a cop car, poking my lipstick and tampons and compact with a pen, all careful, as if I might be carrying something deadly to the Golden Corral on Mother's Day. I knew what they were looking for. "I don't use drugs," I said. "And I don't carry weapons. And that little bottle you're rolling around there, that's liquid Tylenol for my baby." They just gave me the shut-up-you-piece-of-shit stare.

Then I saw them leading Jerry out, cuffed. They leaned him against a car and started asking him questions. I turned to the cop. "That woman knocked my kid down," I said.

"That so?" the cop said. And he started going through my billfold counting out the twelve dollars then going through my change. "I heard you punched that old lady."

I nodded, made sure he put the money back and said, "She knocked my baby down. Surely someone in there saw that."

He shrugged. "We're questioning everyone in the place. You'd be better off keeping your mouth shut." So I stood there thinking how I'd be booked for assault, and they'd probably book Jerry, and he'd do time with his record, and my kids, they'd go to some home while I tried to work myself out of another damned mess.

I felt the crying shaking up inside me, and I didn't want to let those gawkers standing out in the parking lot to see me weak because there's nothing more disgusting than to see a piece of trash crying on the street, which is what they would see in me, not a woman staying straight to raise her kids. So I tried that breathing thing Jerry does, in easy, out slow like a hiss. The cop gave me a look. "I'm just breathing," I said, and with the way he looked at me you'd think that was a crime.

Then I went easy when I saw my boys being led to the grassy island where they plant things in front of The Home Depot. I was happy to see that at least they got ice cream cones, and the cops were being gentle with them, putting their monster trucks in the grass and trying to get them to play. Jessie got to rolling his truck over the ground. But Tyler kept shifting his eyes from the cop and to me and to the cop again. I knew he wanted to run for me, so I gave him the thumbs up sign. He gave me the thumbs up back, but I could see his arm shaking a little, just enough so only a mother would know. "It's okay, Tyler," I called. "Just play with your truck over there." One of the cops gave him a little nudge, put his truck in his hand, but he just sat and stared at me. I could see the ice cream melting down his hand. He threw it on the ground and made a move to come toward me, but I didn't want anyone to stop him, any more crying, any more of anything that would draw a bigger crowd. So I called, "Tyler, see if you can find a four-leaf clover over there." And he stood there like he was thinking about it. I said, "Go on, Tyler. We could use the luck."

That got him going. He turned to the ground and studied it, moving his hands through the grass. And I knew there wasn't a chance in hell he'd find anything, but at least he'd stay busy for a while.

Then a cop came out from the restaurant, and headed toward me. "Miss," he called, "We've got your boys settled, but your girl won't quit crying in there. Any thing we can do?"

I said, "She wants her momma." He nodded like he might do something to satisfy me and turned to go back in. Then another cop came over, and said, "Miss Jenkins, you mind telling me why you punched that woman."

I said it again. "She knocked down my baby girl."

He shook his head. "That's just a little hard to believe given she's a sixty-two year old Christian woman who needs a walker to get across a room." And I thought of that fat lady with a cross as big as a fist dangling between her big old boobs hanging down to her waist, and I started to say something about she only needed a walker to help hold her fat ass off the ground, but I swallowed the words. "And you," the detective said, looking at my worn-out face, then at my too-short skirt and my toenails that needed painting. "Well, you know who you are."

I knew he'd pulled up my record for DUI's and that one bar fight. So I said, "I'm the mother of those kids. And I'm telling you that woman knocked my child down. Do you have kids, officer? What would you do if someone knocked down your kid who isn't even two yet?"

He just shook his head and walked away.

I saw the cop bringing Lacey Dawn to me, and I ran for her and somehow the cops let me, and then I was standing there with her trying to hold me, but my hands were cuffed. And before I could holler, please, a cop got the cuffs off, and I was holding my girl. She put her head to my chest and made these choking little sounds, the crying all cried out. I felt the heat of her and saw her pull at her ear. "She's fighting an ear infection," I said. I looked over at my purse on top of the car. "Could somebody bring me that bottle of Tylenol? That's what she needs. If it weren't Mother's Day, I'd get her to the doctor."

"We have an ER at the hospital," the cop said. "Plenty of mothers like you take their kids there." Then I felt the old fury at the words: "mothers like you." In my drinking days I would have let him have it, and been locked up again. But I was sober. I closed my eyes, breathed the sweet sweaty smell of Lacey Dawn.

"She has a doctor," I said softly. "We like her doctor. I thought we could just get through Mother's Day. I've been to ER. Sometimes you're in there eight hours before they have a look at you." He nodded and looked back toward the crowd slowly coming out of the building.

"If you could bring me her Tylenol and maybe something cold for her to drink. She likes their lemonade." He looked up at me, seemed to like the plan. He got my purse and told another cop to get the lemonade.

I held her to my chest, and looked over, saw they still had Jerry cuffed. "He didn't do anything wrong," I said. The detective just nodded, kept his eye on the crowd trickling out, gawking at us standing until the cops shooed them off to get into their cars and go home. Lacey Dawn took her Tylenol easy. She likes taking drops because we pretend she's a baby bird and I'm the momma bird feeding her.

Finally I saw the group of Christians come out. The preacher was talking with a detective and when he pointed at me, his followers stood there and nodded their heads. Then the preacher and the detective walked toward me. I saw the boys watching, and Lacey Dawn went still. Finally the preacher spoke. "Officer, we are all sinners here."

The detective said, "Okay, Pastor. But only some of us have broken the law." The preacher reached and patted my arm. There was warmth in his hand. The detective explained how the preacher had seen the woman knock the child to the floor, and that others had seen it too. The preacher nodded.

The cop said, "So we have a series of assaults here."

The preacher stood tall and said, "This woman was protecting her child. A mother is supposed to protect her child."

Then the detective broke in and said the woman inside offered not to press charges if—he jerked his head at me like I was the bad dog on the street—"If that one," he said, "doesn't press charges." Then he pointed toward Jerry. "And that one, he was just restraining the woman in there. No harm done. Just a legal restraint hold." He looked at me. "So, willing to drop charges?" I nodded. The detective sighed and said, "Looks like we're done here."

The cop put his hands on his hips looked at the other cops all waiting for some kind of direction. "Oh hell," he said. "Let's get this place cleared out." They took the cuffs off Jerry, but still stood around him as if he could still be a danger.

Then Tyler hollered, "I found it!" He stood and rushed toward me.

I crouched down to see what had to be some kind of miracle in his hand. He shoved the clover in my face. "See," he said. A four-leaf clover." He looked up at the cops, back to me. I could see worry in his eyes. "Are we lucky yet?"

I took the clump of leaves from his fingers, and he squealed, "You have to hold it real tight." I felt the two stems, the trick I'd used of tearing two leaves off one clover and jamming it against three to make four. I guess it's only a natural thing for any kid to want to make a mother proud. I looked at him, saw the smile forced on his face. He knew I knew the trick. But I would not be my mother. "Yes," I said. "We're lucky now, Tyler."

"Good Lord," the detective said as he walked away. He waved his arms. "Everybody just clear out and go home."

Then the fat lady and her mother came out of the restaurant. She stood leaning on that walker and stared at me. The preacher patted my arm as if to hold me steady. She shook her head and lumbered off.

The preacher said, "I suggest you go home and give thanks for this day."

"I will," I said, and I wanted to tell him you got no idea of my day. I was feeling that old anger stirring again at how some people can just walk by trouble and others just can't help but fall in. But I felt Tyler tugging at my hand. "Are we really lucky now?" I could hear my mother's words snap: *You can't fake your luck, Vickie!* I bent to Tyler, pulled him to me, kissed his head and said. "Sometimes we make our luck, Tyler. Sometimes we have to look and work real hard, but sometimes we can make our luck, even if we have to tear it from the ground."

I looked up and saw Jerry sweep up Jesse in his arms, come toward me. "We are lucky," I said and I kissed Lacey Dawn. "We are lucky," I said again, and told myself to keep saying those words until I could really feel them to be true.

A Taste of Gianni Mascarpone, Please

Lizzy sat in the parking lot of the Spring Meadows mall and stared at the bright lights ahead beckoning with in-door fountains gushing into streams kept running by hidden pumps and copper tubes, plastic plants reaching toward skylights, and perpetual clearance sales. On dark winter nights the mall offered an oasis of warmth and light. And Gianni.

He ran the chocolate shop and was always happy to see her. When Lizzy saw his old handsome Italian face smiling, that gleam in his eye as if he knew her secrets and kept them wrapped in golden foil, she sighed with a relief that was quite simply barbitual. Gianni. She couldn't remember his last name, could only recall it was something like mascarpone, the essential ingredient for her favorite desert of layered cookies and chocolate and cream.

Lizzy leaned forward and checked her face in the mirror. In the dim overhead light, her face looked back asking, "Are you ready?"

"Never," she said as she opened the door, stepped on the pavement, and slipped a bit in her Italian boots too stylish for Ohio winters.

Above her the moon waxed full. Superstitious about such things, Lizzy knew she had one night to begin something because once the moon passed fullness, it was time to wrap things up, harvest those seeds of potential she usually let die. The last time Lizzy made love, it was a crescent moon waning. She remembered it precisely, the man rode her, hunched down and pumping like a jockey urging his thoroughbred to the finish line. His face shadowed in darkness, his hands gripped her shoulders for leverage as she sank deeper into the upholstery of his car. She squeezed her thighs against his hips, knowing the pressure would help make him come faster, and the exercise would help tone her legs. She looked up through the moon roof to the clear night sky and noticed the trees shuddering softly in the high autumn breeze. She watched the slivered bit of the moon. It was a season of completion, things coming to an end.

But now it was winter, and a dome of cold had descended on the city, sealing it in a black ice glaze that made sudden moves dangerous. Struggling to endure, she resorted to desperate measures, her methods for pleasure limited by her weakness for booze and men. A recovering drunk, a recovering Catholic, a recovering recovery, she was coming to believe that life was nothing but a process of trading addictions and you simply had to be careful with your choice.

Lizzy beeped the car locked, hurried across the parking lot, pushed through the revolving door, and entered into a warmth almost tropical. Surrounding the illuminated fountain, bronze sculpted fish eternally gurgled water from their grotesque open mouths. She didn't get it. Was it supposed to make shoppers feel exotic, as if they were in some foreign land? Was the gurgling from a fish mouth some kind of symbol to inspire them to spend as if money spurted perpetually from magical underground streams? Lizzy turned away and unwrapped herself from the scarf, the gloves, the hat, the coat—like armor to survive dangerous weather. She stamped the crusted ice from her boots and watched two teenaged lovers staring at the pulsing arc of spray as if it meant something. Old faithful maybe, that natural geyser that was losing its oomph in a world that was just getting too tired.

Lizzy liked to watch young lovers. The jet-black-haired girl stood tall in her stacked platform shoes, chin up, boobs out, ass a perfect mound—a genetically engineered sex machine, packed into a short thin black skirt and pink T-shirt emblazoned with "Hole." Back when Lizzy was the girl's age, going bra-less was enough to send preachers screeching on the moral decline of the country and politicians playing on the fear of a liberated nipple. Now girls strode the mall with lips painted the color of plumped-up vaginas. The boy, poor dolt, was clinging on the girl like a drowning man clutching a life raft. Lizzy walked past them as the boy cupped his hand around the girl's hip and stood close behind her in a gesture like affection. Lizzy wondered what such a babe was doing with a kid with his cap on backwards and his pasty face and khaki pants so baggy the crotch hung half to his knees. Lizzy smiled when she saw the girl staring off past the fountain, down the long glaring mall and looking nothing but bored.

Lizzy understood. Although she usually didn't go for small men like the last one, he had lured her with his sharp dark features that reminded her of Al Pacino. She had to admit she missed his long carpenter's fingers that could reach and wriggle inside her to pull orgasms out like dripping thick honeycomb from a buzzing hive. Problem was he could never make her come while they were screwing, and it pissed him off that he couldn't reach her G-spot. He'd insist, "I'm big enough to do it. Where the hell's your G-spot? Hiding up there behind your ribs?" Most guys didn't get it. A woman's G-spot was tucked safely and stubbornly in the dark shadows of her head.

Gianni would understand that. He was the old-style Italian who knew something about women and romance. He had told her long ago, while watching her bite into coconut truffle right there in his store. "It's a sure sign of love, Miss Lizzy, when a man feeds a woman. And I don't mean restaurants like these men these days putting fancy meals on expense accounts just to lure you ladies. No, a man must offer something made with his hands. My wife she taught me that." When Gianni talked of his long dead wife, Lizzy couldn't tell if the tears brimming in his eyes were from sorrow or joy.

Gianni offered chocolates. He didn't make them, but he offered them in little gold foil bags or arranged on white doilies at the center of glossy pink plates. His store was called Sweet Temptations, but Lizzy thought of it as Sweet Substitutions since his fine chocolates could make her feel something like love, something like sex, keep her safely distracted in winter when usually her body became a heat-seeking missile that led her to new lovers whose forced fervor sparked her heart to glow, for a moment. Lizzy knew it was a biochemical response, which in a short time only left her lonely and bored. Still she craved men, the smell of them, the sweet muscled heat of them, big men brought down to writhe with her touch.

When a man came in her mouth, she often thought of chocolate breaking between her teeth, the smooth hard surface spilling sweet spurts of cognacs, brandies, and thick, fruited liqueurs. Why was it everything she had always reminded her of something she didn't? Now she had to satisfy herself with chocolate, that pleasure of the firm silky surface between her teeth, the relief of the breaking on her tongue, the relenting thick cream.

But now her little weekly purchases of chocolates couldn't give her a high. She knew the taste, texture, smell before she unwrapped them, could replay the effect in her brain so well her body couldn't be bothered by the craving.

Again and again she returned to Gianni for new suggestions, but when she got them home they were too sweet, too gooey thick, sticking to her palate like some waxy foreign object that just didn't belong. That's how it was with addiction, no pleasure really, just the wanting to want to relive desire. Her chocolates were stacking up unused now, craved but unwanted. Little gold paper bags lined up on her kitchen shelf, untouched, like all those wineglasses she no longer used.

She wandered down the mall toward Gianni, and was already feeling warmer, softer, as if on vacation with the artificial trees reaching up toward skylights, white trellises wrapped in plastic vines. Lizzy half-expected wind-up parrots to come swooping down and eat caramel popcorn out of shoppers' hands. She walked thinking she should try a new chocolate, something totally different this time. She hoped Gianni could help her, hoped he had something secret on his shelves, some new confection that would satisfy something more than her body's needs.

The mall's clock read two minutes until closing. Was he waiting? Was he worried? Did he remember this was her night for his therapy of truffles and talk? Would he notice, or just stand there humming to himself, mopping up the floor, sealing the door shut to count up the day's cash and go? She hurried, moving as quickly as her high-heeled boots would allow. Surely he was missing her, watching the clock. Please. She ran.

Girls in black clothes wheeled the aromatherapy bar back into The Body Shop. "You're late," one called. Lizzy waved, moved on. Jesus, did everyone in the place know her habit? Was she as pathetic as that? Did they laugh? Inside, the girl bent at the entrance, pressed the button to lower the metal security door.

"Damn." Gianni was all the way down at the other end of the mall. She always parked far away to give herself a walk, to see the sales, and enjoy the light, hoping maybe she'd see someone she knew.

She looked ahead and saw Gianni's shop, the red illuminated letters curling in the kind of script found on valentines. As the bells chimed the signal that the mall was closed, she saw him, her sweet kind Gianni, nodding to a tune in his head as he bent to press the button lowering the door.

"Gianni," she called, running now. He looked up just in time to see her slip on some stranger's spilled hot chocolate. Her back wrenched for balance as her ankle collapsed, and she crumpled to the floor.

"Miss Lizzy!" he called. But she couldn't see him. Her eyes pinched shut as a flame surged up her ankle to her calf. She pulled herself up to sit, gripped her foot and held it. She saw Gianni running toward her. "Miss Lizzy!" Her throat ached, and a knot like a fist was pummeling in her chest. She held tears back, took a breath, exhaled slowly, the way they'd taught her in recovery, to let the pain escape with her breath hissing between clenched teeth.

Gianni bent over her, touched her shoulder, "Let me

help you," he whispered as he took her hand, held her waist, and lifted her up.

"Are you all right?" he kept muttering as he helped her to his shop.

She nodded, let him bear her weight, knowing if she spoke she would sob. She kept her body tight. Tight, she kept thinking, keep it tight. She pushed the hardness knotted in her chest up and out, making it envelop her like hard chocolate, the crust firmly containing an oozing center. She'd be all right if she didn't let the comfort of his touch sink past her skin. She pulled free of him. "Don't touch me." She saw the shock in his face. "Please," she added. "Just don't touch me now, please."

"I'm so sorry," he said, stepping away. "I didn't mean. . . " He busied himself with taking two up-ended chairs off the wooden table. "Sit," he said. "You can rest here." He turned and pressed the button. "You sit. I only come to help you," he said keeping his eyes on the lowering metal door.

"I'm sorry," she said. "It's just if you touch me, I'll cry."

He glanced back at her and moved toward his counter. "Can I bring you something? Water? An espresso? A hot cocoa. It will soothe you."

She balanced on the chair and lifted her aching foot to rest it on her knee. She could feel it throbbing, swelling already under the boot.

"You need ice. Get that silly boot off, and I bring you something." He headed toward the back room. "You shouldn't run. What in heaven is a grown woman doing running, shoes like that, running down a mall?"

"You were closing." Tears were squeaking up. "Oh God," she moaned.

He returned with a plastic bag filled with ice. "I would have opened for you, Miss Lizzy." He looked back toward his chocolate case, waved his hand. "I know you have need for your chocolate. I understand." He patted her shoulder. "You are my most loyal customer." He smiled. "And this old heart flutters like a dove when you walk in my store."

He put the bag of ice on the table and turned to go back behind his counter. "Get that silly boot off. I make something to soothe you."

She watched him work with the espresso machine. "Gianni, I've got to tell you something. " He paused, looked back. She straightened. "You know all those little bags of chocolate I buy here. Every week I come, take your advice, select three perfect chocolates, carry them home. I haven't eaten them for a month. They sit lined up on my kitchen shelf. I can't drink, I can't date, and now I don't know why, but I can't even eat chocolate." She kept staring at her boot, her throbbing ankle, felt the heat swelling under the finely stitched seams. "I come here," she said. "I have to come here. But I don't want them. They're too sweet, too thick, too something." She glanced up at him, watching her with his arms across his chest and softly nodding.

"I just don't want them," Lizzy said. Oh God, she was whining.

"*O Dio mio*. This is worse than I thought," he said shoving napkins in her hands, pretty little designer napkins, borders printed with roses and unfurling green vines.

She stared at the roses. "It's so lonely. I sit in my dark little apartment, eating those damned chocolates by myself. I'm pathetic, Gianni." She kept her eyes on the roses, took her breath, tried to bring her voice back down to a normal range, but it kept slipping up again. "It was all I had, Gianni, my only pleasure, and now I don't want that. I don't want anything, Gianni. Nothing. How can you live when you don't want anything at all?"

"Elizabeth," he said, sitting beside her. "You want

everything. I know this. This is the only reason you are so sad. Wanting everything can only lead to a broken heart."

She glanced up. He had never called her Elizabeth before. That was what her father had called her. "Elizabeth, a name fit for a queen," he had said. But her father was dead; her mother was dead. The mall was closed and the whole world was dead, except for Gianni who now looked at her with such kindness she was trembling. If he kept offering kindness, she'd soften, melt, and ooze like a caramel cream candy left too long in the sun.

Lizzy stared at the gleaming leather of her boot, knew she should take it off, but she'd never squeeze her foot back in that tight leather. She could see herself limping, like a bag lady in the darkness, toward her car.

"But your ankle is the only problem at the moment. And it's very simple. You want no pain in your ankle, and this we can fix." He pushed the bag of ice toward her. "Now take that boot off and let me see what you have done to yourself." She carefully began pulling down the zipper while he held the ice bag ready. "Easy," he whispered. He shook his head, "You silly young women wearing these designer boots in winter."

"They're good boots," she said. "Italian."

"I know they are Italian. You have the good sense to buy quality shoes, yes. But you young women." He watched her tenderly unzip the boot. "You try to look so sexy every day like sexy is some uniform. Sexy." He paused, leaned back, smiled. "My wife. She knew. Sexy is a thing to be saved. Like Christmas lights. No one would brighten at the sight of Christmas lights if we strung them all the year. *Capisc?*" He stood and shook his head as she pulled off the boot exposing her stockinged foot pink and already going purple. "Look at those pitiful pinched toes." He placed the ice across her ankle and turned away. "When you are old you'll have bunions so big, you'll waddle like my old grandma in Italy." He crouched, squinched his face into a frown, and shuffled toward his counter. "You want to grow old like that?" He pointed to her foot. "You ruin those feet, the only feet you have this whole life. When you grow old, very sad, every step will hurt, you keep living like this."

She pressed the ice against her throbbing ankle, tried to see herself as old. "Gianni," she whispered without looking up, "you really think I'll be old one day? You really think I'll live long?"

He turned away. "I can't promise you that." She saw him pause, take a breath as he bent at the machine. "But you don't need to be old to grow a full life. My wife, we grew more love in fifteen years than most do in a lifetime." He flipped a switch, and a cloud of steam erupted with a hard hiss. She watched his back, his strong broad back, his body solid, thick with appetite. His wife, she must have loved this man. He turned to Lizzy with a cup, gently stirring. "What you need is some of my fresh cocoa. Ghirardelli. The best. My cocoa it takes tenderness, stirring, patience." He nodded to her. "You sit, be patient." He added more steamed milk to her cup and stirred. "You Americans. So in a hurry. So living in the future, you see only where you want to be instead of where you are." He turned, shook his finger, and smiled. "That is how you fall down, Miss Lizzy. Now wait, my chocolate will soothe you."

She eased back in her chair, closed her eyes, and listened to the spoon clinking against the cup. She heard him humming something, something foreign she figured. How could a man be so happy, his wife gone, grown children gone, living some West Coast high-tech life outside LA. She opened her eyes and watched the glowing light of the candy case, studied the chocolates arranged on doilies on the glass shelves lined with pink paper. There wasn't much in there she hadn't tried.

Gianni came toward her with a white china cup and saucer, placed it gently on the table, and sat. "My chocolate, I make the best, homemade, old style, real cocoa, fresh milk. You Americans have no business ruining a fine thing with these little powered packets, dried milk, chemicals, and water just zapped in some microwave." He sat back and sighed. "It is no way to live I tell you."

Lizzy stared at the ridiculous mound of whipped cream. "That's pure fat!"

"See, Gianni has you smiling now. Life isn't so sad. And you need a little fat on those bird bones." He lightly circled her wrist with his fingers and placed her hand gently back on the table. "A miracle you don't break like glass when you fall."

Balanced on the edge of her saucer was a thin wafer of dark chocolate. He pointed. "This one you haven't tried. Very nice. Delicate. In Italy, we serve these with espresso, cappuccino, cocoa. Such good warm things deserve a little extra on the side. We all deserve a little extra. The *dolce vita*," he smiled. "The sweet life. The good life. You Americans work so hard at living. Even for pleasure you have to take some class at some school. Go pay good money, study happiness someplace. As if God didn't give you the gift. No you have to go buy it in some mall, take lessons somewhere." He sighed and shook his head. "This, Miss Lizzy, is a sad thing. I feel for this country."

Lizzy nodded, not speaking of the yoga lessons, tai chi, facial treatments, massage, vibrators, the prices paid for someone, something to help her feel her own body's potential for pleasure in being alive. She sipped the silky warm milk, the whipped cream kissing her upper lip with coolness. She licked her lips. "Heavenly, Gianni," she said dipping her head to inhale the sweet warmth. "All this time I've come to you, and never tried this."

"My wife," he smiled. "She said she married me for my cooking. And all the time I told her, 'Not for my good looks?'" He laughed, shook his head, and she saw tears glistening in his dark eyes.

Lizzy patted his hand. "Your wife knows you miss her. I'm sure she knows."

Gianni nodded. "Of course, but I have her still here. She's here." He tapped the center of his chest. Lizzy wanted to lay her head there, listen to that strong heart. "She tells me," Gianni said, "she whispers, 'Be happy Gianni, life is sweet. It is there for you to go on and enjoy.'" He straightened, smiled. "And I believe her." He reached and squeezed her shoulder. "There is a saying you can learn, Miss Lizzy. Sorrow looks back, worry looks around, but faith looks up." He pointed up and said. "Look up, Lizzy." She did and saw only the rose-colored ceiling, a thin crack in the plaster growing across the center of the room.

He pushed her cup closer. "You haven't tried your chocolate. Never overlook the free little extras. Most days they sit right in front of you, and you go on looking someplace in the future, missing what is right there."

"I told you, Gianni. That's my problem. I don't even want chocolate anymore." She stared at the wafer balanced on her saucer. "Maybe I should switch to pretzels. They're no-fat."

'*Macche*,' Gianni shook his head. "Nonsense. A woman needs chocolate. I've seen books on this thing. A woman, her body, it needs chocolate." He smiled. "Go on."

She looked at the wafer, wondered why she'd never tried one before.

"Trust me," he said. "It isn't too sweet, not bitter, just good." He held the chocolate up toward her face.

She opened her mouth and let him place the wafer on her tongue. She closed her lips and let the chocolate break, melt, instantly merging with the wet warmth of her mouth. It wasn't like eating, but a soft coalescing, an instant sensation of pleasure felt, tasted, gone.

He smiled and squeezed her hand. "Tastes like *amore*, no?"

She smiled. "It's like communion," she said. "That's what the holy host should be, Gianni. More people would stay with the church."

He grinned, stood, moving toward the back of the store. "Think I should write the pope?"

She laughed, looked out at the darkened mall. An old Sting song was still playing on the mall's sound system, the one about everything a girl does being magic. "You're better than a therapist," she called. "You are a magician."

Gianni returned with a white towel, took the ice bag off her ankle, and wrapped the towel around her foot.

She leaned back and closed her eyes. "You are the kindest man I've ever known."

"Maybe you've known the wrong ones. You young women these days. Everyone fussing. Women saying men are so bad. Men saying women are crazy. When did men and women go to war? They argue; they fight; they write books; they say we come from other planets. This is silly talk." He sat back and looked around his store. "We are human, Miss Lizzy. All humans just looking for some bit of love before we die." He paused, hands gripping the table. "Most men, Elizabeth, we love women. Really."

Lizzy looked at his handsome puzzled face and laughed as tears came rising, tears for all those men who had plunged inside her, in and out and in and out and gone. It seemed she'd never really spoken to a one of them. Here in the soft rose light of Gianni's shop she felt she'd spent her life living like a reptile, driven by appetite, slinking up from moist heat, to a thrusting of silent muscle, then slinking back away to a slick dark river, moving silently, secretly along. "Oh Gianni," she said, "why can't I meet a man like you?"

"But you have," he said, stroking her hair.

She sank her head into his touch and closed her eyes. She leaned into him, feeling him like a lover, a father, a mother, someone nameless, timeless, a soothing steady touch of love.

He was kissing the top of her head. In the dark mall, the music suddenly shut off. Silence, just the dim glow of the chocolate case, a comforting steady hum. She lifted her face up, let him kiss her, a full kiss, a warm kiss, a kissing that wasn't demanding hunger, but rather just was another way of talking, a sweet silent syntax of pressure, easing back, searching out again.

They pulled back and looked straight at each other smiling. "Gianni," Lizzy said. "Are you superstitious?"

He shrugged. "I believe in magic. Even miracles sometimes." He took her hand, kissed it.

She sighed and looked up to the ceiling. "The moon is full tonight, Gianni. This means something. A completion of things begun." She paused, touched his face. "This began a long time ago."

He shook his head and kissed her palm.

"Gianni, listen. I'm serious," she said. "The moon is full. I know it. Above this ceiling, this roof of steel, above the parking lot lights, way above that cold dark freezing night out there, the moon is full. This is a completion, a good thing."

He pulled back, looked at her, and laughed. "The moon is always full, Miss Elizabeth. It never changes. This full moon, half moon, crescent moon, you young ones talk about in all your new age books. It's silliness. Think about it. You say the moon changes shape, but what you see is only a reflection of light." He took her hand, pulled her closer, "The sun, the moon are always there in fullness." He kissed her forehead. "Even in the dark," he whispered. "Nothing really goes away." He pulled her closer until she leaned into his chest, sank into his heat, his heartbeat, his breath.

She looked up into his warm and happy face and thought, it all goes away, Gianni. But she wouldn't say it, not to him. He believed in things like love. He believed hurts were healed with care and hungers could be satisfied. "Please kiss me," she said. And he did. He kissed her softly, deeply then. And she fed on his taste of chocolate and cream, wanting to be in his life, wanting to know his heart, to breathe his breath, hoping if she could visit his world long enough, she could find a way to stay.

Calypso

I stand naked at the window, waiting, while he goes to the lobby to call his wife. We were kissing when she buzzed him on his cell phone, his tongue soft and pushing in my mouth, his wool jacket scratchy on my breasts. He says he likes the vibration better than the ring and he gives that goofy grin the way boys in high school do. Thing is, he's old. But there it was, I felt the bzzz of her calling in his pocket. He jumped, glanced at the dull green light of the illuminated number, looked twice as if surprised. He gave me a light kiss on my forehead, shrugged, said his wife was no doubt checking to see when he'd be home. But it often happens, so I wonder why he acts surprised.

I wait, like always when he slips off to make his calls. I

watch the cars out there in the early darkness. Winter darkness, creeping toward the shortest day of the year. Streams of cars keep moving down the road all bright with strip malls, service stations, fast food signs. Some drivers slow down, pull in the huge movie parking lot out there just below me. The drivers rev and break and rev and break as they search for open spaces closest to the entrance of the Cineplex where they show six movies at a time. I breathe on the glass to see my breath bead on the window. "Hel-lo," I say to no one. They can't see me up here in the dark room of the Comfort Inn. They have no idea. I could sing to them, cry to them, and no one would hear me. "Hel-lo."

Quiet headlights beam soft rays in the darkness, turn signals blink, and brake lights flare. I press my ear to the cold glass, listen to the sound of car doors opening, clicking shut, people laughing, shouting, talking, couples, families, little clumps of friends. It's cold out, the kind of cold that freezes in your nose when you breathe. They tighten their scarves and hurry toward the warmth and light and popcorn. They're happy, knowing they're about to be lifted by some vision on a screen, white light from the projection booth beaming them to a timeless place where dying isn't really dying, where kisses can be replayed to be fresh and longing always. Suddenly I'm tired.

I press my face, my nipples against the cold glass. I like the way it wakes me while the soft warm tufts of air blow up from the hotel heater, warm my belly, soothe my thighs. I stretch my arms wide to hold the window frame, listen for the sound of him returning. He likes to find me naked, to see me like a nymph, he says, savor the raw sweet loveliness of me. He uses words like that, romantic words, like in a movie where violins are playing, where there's a crying for joy or sadness, something of consequence at the end.

I call him my professor, but he isn't really mine. He just looked so the type that day I met him. He's an older man. I don't mean old, old, but something more like my father's age. Grown up, used to jackets, ties, socks that match his pants, polished lace-up shoes. He came in the coffee bar one day with his tie loose, his jacket open and the kind of jazzy briefcase only a professor type would use. "What's your pleasure, professor?" I said. He gave me a long look, the way men do when I take their coffee order like that. Men like my mouth, my thick black hair, my smiling dark blue eyes. Most times my "what's your pleasure" gets a dollar dropped into the tip jar, a little conversation, something to help the day go by, but never quite like he did. "My pleasure," he sighed, eyes quickly moving over the board's selection of coffee drinks, then circling back to me. "My pleasure," he said again, gaze dropping to my breasts, which always get attention. He smiled straight into my face. "My pleasure," he said one more time, "I do believe it's you." He stared as if waiting for an answer, had these hard dark eyes, so big and bright they should be soft and kind, but they're hard in a way you don't see on boys, can freeze you, make your heart race while the air goes still.

So we did it that night. He had a way of wanting me that made it easy to say yes. He still laughs and makes jokes about the Comfort Inn—him being the weary traveler seeking comfort. He likes to make things stories, but I know we picked the Comfort Inn because it's closest to the coffee bar, so when I got off work I could walk right over. Easy, quick and, for him I guess, relatively cheap.

The first night it was sort of fast and hard and desperate with his tongue jabbing in and in my mouth so fast I couldn't really kiss him back while his hands pulled off my clothes. He crawled over licking, nibbling, kissing me, his tongue and fingers, cock so quick in and out and in and staying hard forever. I felt like a butter churn with him in and out while my insides frothed up pure white cream. When we were finished he turned the lights on bright just to look at me. He kneeled on the bed, stared down at me while I tried to guess his age, the lined skin at his throat, the crinkles at the corners of his eyes, the hair receding, black giving way to gray. I asked him then, "Is your hair what they call salt and pepper?" I'd always heard salt and pepper was a color, never thought I'd see it nuzzling at my breasts, feel it thin and coarse between my fingers.

He paused, then took a breath. He ran his hands over his hair, his face went blank, and then he seemed to make a choice to laugh. He bent over me, crouched with his hands at my shoulders, knees straddling my hips. "You are such an innocent," he said, and he took my hand and gave me this wet warm open kiss right there in the center of my palm. "And that is what I like, you're such a child."

I wanted to laugh, say I was no virgin. I'd sucked boys off and done things. I wanted to tell him I really was a gifted child, that I was reading grown up books at ten. I had looked up words like loins and lechery while other girls were playing with smooth-crotched dolls. But he kept kissing, sucking at my palm like he was sipping something from me. A shiver rippled up my arm, and I felt some old connection as if my blood had known this man, as if kisses were some strange return. I wanted him then, not like the way I wanted him before we did it, just wanting to try something new. I wanted his pure wanting me, went happy and excited the way my puppy gets when I come home from school and he stands at the door just quivering, knowing I'll bend to pet and give him soft warm scratches, rubs, and love.

It's been three months since then.

The doors clicks open, and he shakes his head, says he

can't believe I take the risk of standing naked at the window—even though we both know it's something he asks. But it isn't such a risk as long as I stand in darkness—there'd only be a danger if I flipped on the light. I know enough to know that those in darkness can't see into darkness. Like his wife.

He takes off his watch and wedding band, reaches for his phone to put on the bedside table and a business card drops to the floor. He sweeps to pick it up, gives it a glance, and slips it in his pocket. He shrugs and smiles. When boys shrug like that, they're lying somehow, dodging something small, but big in irritation. I know this, wonder now, wonder what he sees when he looks at me, wonder what I'm doing here, who I am as I turn in a pose I know he likes.

"You, my dear, are a vision," he says, now coming toward me. He stands fully clothed in front of me the way he likes to be at the start, me naked, him in his jacket, slacks and shirt, the loosened tie. He smiles until I grin and turn my face up for his kiss, and he reaches behind and runs his hands over the small of my back, fingers circling slowly down to grab my ass and lift me up and into a firm and steady squeeze. He doesn't kiss like boys who move their light tongues like humming birds, dipping darting as if they have to sneak. He sucks softly like I'm pudding on a spoon, running his mouth over the soft thick flesh of me, lightly taking surface for the texture then coming back with a little more pressure to take a deeper taste, pulling, sucking, tasting, again, again until I'm cool cream pudding disappearing not in one clean bite but a kind of melting down.

I pause, pull back to nibble at his neck, to smell the wool of his jacket, his cotton, soap scent so different from the boys who smell like trees and sweat and summer grass. The professor smells instead like paper, fabric, motel rooms and glass. "There," he says. "Let me look at you." He steps away, and I pose, clasp my hands as if playing coy to hide my naked crotch while he admires the thick sloping of my breasts, the roundness of my ass. He likes my body. He often says he loves it. Most boys say I'm plump—the boys my age they like the skinny kind with long straight thighs and bodies thin and hard with little ice cream scoops for breasts.

"A vision," he says again, now backing up as if I were a painting. "A living moving timeless image of just ripe womanhood caught in a contemporary frame." I don't know how he can see me really in the dim room, lit barely by the bathroom light. He likes to talk things like images and visions. He says I signify things I'm too young to understand. He likes to make simple things sound complex and deep and grand.

And sometimes I believe him. His words can slip inside my head the way he pushes his cock between my legs. Something of him always stays inside me. His words, his sweat and breath and cum, it sticks and seeps inside my cells to become a little part of who I am. It's one of the things I like about screwing him—he'd call it *making love*, or *human mingling, merging*, something mythic, deep and fine.

He looks at my face, cups it in his hand for a closer look. "What was that look you just gave me?"

"What?" I say. I rub my arms, try to turn away and tell him I'm just cold.

"Cold, precisely" he says, as he pulls the drapes closed. "I'll have to be careful not let my little love get cold."

His little love. The words should make me laugh. The boys would never call me little; my girlfriends say I'm petite but just a little plump. His little love, like a lucky trinket small enough to fit into his pocket, hidden in the darkness with the lint. I see the way he looks at me, remember some things do have greater value for diminished size, like a bonsai tree or a miniature pony. Suddenly I want to be outside. I want to see a movie, eat fast food with my friends.

He wraps his arms around me, pulls me close and whispers, "Are you warming now?"

Before I can answer, he bends and takes my breast in his mouth, and he sucks until I have to let him hold me while my body rises, my center weakens, and I feel gravity move above me as if it were a force that lifted instead of holding down. He pulls me to the bed, and I let him because there's a pleasure in being sucked and swallowed like a ripe warm peach. This is what he gives me. He's nothing like the other boys who pick and nibble at me like I'm some fresh warm box of popcorn being passed around. He savors, swallows, smiles as if I were a nice steak hot and laced with pepper and smoking straight from the grill. I pull him down to me, and like the rough feel of his jacket, the crisp feel of his shirt against my skin, the belt buckle cool and hard on my belly. He pulls back and lightly kisses each of my nipples then he smiles at me and says, "You think I'm old?"

He's smiling, but I can see he's crying somewhere. The older men in the coffee shop, they do this sometimes, watch me as if I'm the last rosy-fingered sunset they'll ever see. He goes to the mirror and with his palm brushes his hair back while he sucks in his breath a little, raises his chin and looks at his neck as if he's looking for some sign of something, some dangerous new sag or line.

"I have something new to show you," he says now, switching on the lamp and turning to his briefcase. "This is who you are." He pulls out an art book—he always has to teach me something when we meet. He says he wants to teach me how traditional myths unconsciously shape my vision of the world—as if this world is something I don't know.

"Okay," I say as he flips to a page marked with a yellow sticky note. He sits on the end of the bed and pats the mattress beside him. I nestle at his shoulder and lean to see a picture of a man, a hero-type, half-clothed, looking mournful as he turns to hear a winged messenger whispering at his ear, while his body leans still toward a woman with such shape and skin tones, she can't be simply human. I read this myth in AP-English: the wandering warrior meets the temptress, loves and longs to stay, but aches to go.

"Odysseus," the professor says, "And his Calypso. After the Trojan war, he was trying to get home, but Poseidon had his reasons and wrecked the ship. Odysseus swam on Calypso's island where she fed him, warmed him, loved him until the gods decided he had to return home."

"Stop," I say. "I know the story." But I pull the book closer to see Calypso's face. I want to see if she's really as calm, indifferent as the story suggests.

The professor points, "See how Odysseus longs to lean closer and yet pulls away?" He shakes his head and sighs, "Duty, pleasure, pain."

I look at Calypso's face, her milk white skin like mine, her woman's shape, the muscles at her calves, her feet that seem too small to carry all her weight, her quiet curving strength. And I know this is why he wants me. He thinks I am a nymph, he thinks I am a witch, he thinks that I'm a wild exotic flower blooming succulent in a private cave. He doesn't know I see something simple and eternal as dust and dirt and water. He's an educated man, but he sees only flowers, not the thick black dirt beneath.

Calypso knows. She probably screws Odysseus until he's crying, and she doesn't even sweat. She knows what she is and wants. She'll long outlast this weeping, whining man who looks somehow both sad and relieved to hear the messenger fluttering at his ear with news he has to go. She knows this man is leaving, but she doesn't really mind. Only an immortal could have a man for seven years then help him build his raft to send him sailing home.

"Poor Odysseus," my professor says as he reaches and closes the book and leans to me. He whispers, "You are my Calypso." I close my eyes and let him kiss me because when he's kissing me, he forgets to talk and I'm so tired of words.

He covers me with his body, holds my face between his hands and thrusts, thrusts his tongue in the big soft way that always makes me throb, even when I don't really want him. And I think maybe this is how Odysseus felt melting in her arms. Maybe I'm the captive; maybe the professor is the witch. Maybe it's a choice the way we play. Then he slips his fingers inside me, mouth sucking at my breast, and my body slips and quivers.

"I'm going to prepare for you," he says, standing, leaving me wanting him to just do it. He turns to the bathroom where he'll take a shower, to emerge a cloud of steam. I watch him brighten for a moment in the yellow light of the bathroom before he closes the door. See him one last moment in his professor clothes, remember he's got a wife and kids, things like mortgages, retirements plans, college funds. I pick up the book and read: *Rubens' Gods and Goddesses.* I remember seeing a TV show on how aristocrats once liked to dress up like immortals and have their portraits painted. I flip through the pages, see the usual gods and goddesses, wonder about the models, who they really were. My professor thinks I'm innocent. He doesn't know I'm gifted. I've had a love of words so strong, they called it an obsession; they advised a break from school to let my emotions catch up with what my brain knew. They said I needed time to adjust to an older peer group. He doesn't know I've always been advanced. There's a lot he doesn't know.

Like he doesn't know I have his private number, and I can call his wife. I slipped from the bed once after he was snoring. I sneaked with his billfold into the bathroom, ran my fingers through the credit cards, receipts and things until I found something with his number on the ID card that says if found please return, there'd be a cash reward. All I wanted was a number for his home. I wanted to know his wife's voice, the sound of his children, the simple noise of his daily life. He's told me her name is Helen. A classic name, and he says she's a classic bitch. But he says a lot of things. He doesn't know I've heard her voice, not a bitch voice, just a woman's voice wondering at the moment's silence when I called. I've only called her once, but I replay that private moment, two women connected by a fiber optic line while the man between them dreams of mythic things and snores.

I study Calypso's face looking back at me, and I see she knows how it is to be the one caught in a frozen moment, lifted out of time, lifted out of the history of man-made things like kitchens, kids, and wives with lives attached to time. I've never heard of Calypso being jealous, never heard of her wanting Penelope's life of looms and tending daily fires. She was an immortal. She knew the man would come and go while she lived on in a larger life. I look into Calypso's eyes, blow her a kiss through the air between us, feel some connection hold.

I put his book on the table, listen for the sound of him showering, and I wonder what he washes off. The scent of someone else's sex, or the smell of growing old? He keeps me waiting always, the way he keeps his wife waiting, holding dinner late, the way I'm sure he keeps his students waiting, watching the clock, wondering if and when he'll enter, start the class.

I hear the shower stop, imagine him now a little pink, glistening in the steam. I sit up on the edge of the bed, my feet on the floor and my body turned toward him the way I know he likes. I think of Calypso, how her hips turn toward the man, thighs slightly parted, while her face turns away to say hello to whoever might be watching, as if to say, "It's all right. I was getting tired of him really, with his standing at the shoreline nightly sighing, wanting this and that and this and that as if options were a torture and not a gift."

I look at the clock. The early movies are halfway done by now. My friends will be there soon, lining up and laughing to see the later show. They'll do the movie, then go grab burgers at the drive-thru, go somewhere else to sit and smoke and dance. If I hurried I could join them. I'm sixteen, and I'm sitting here waiting for a man with salt and pepper hair. I could be my mother. I could be his wife. I could be another woman he fits into his life. I wonder at the phone call now, that number on the phone, the second glance, the little lying shrug. I reach and run my hand in the pocket of his jacket, find the business card. *Evelyn Murphy*, it says. *Realtor.* I study the number circled, not with a circle, but with a heart. There are lots of numbers, but this is a special one she wanted him to have. I reach for the phone, push the button to illuminate the last number called, not his private number, but the Evelyn Murphy woman, another grown-up in his life. A woman who draws hearts on things, like the stupid girls at school. I shove the card back in his pocket, hurry to arrange myself on the bed as he steps from the bathroom and pauses in the dim light, whirling steam.

"My sweet Calypso," he whispers as he steps across the room. He holds me now with warm damp arms, kisses my neck with the way that makes me shiver, makes me rise to the pull of his mouth, his breath, his arms. I hear him whisper, "Calypso luring me with pleasures in her sweet dark cave." I push him back and say my name is Katy. A sadness moves over his face. "Katy, then," he says. He takes my hand and kisses the center of my palm, the way I know he'll suck soon at my breast, the way he'll lap and suck between my thighs. This is the way he does things; this is the way he loosens all my muscles, veins and bones inside and sends me liquid spilling like warm red wine.

He pulls then, pushes me down on the bed and takes my breast in his mouth, while his fingers push inside and I feel the rush of heat, mouth, breasts, belly, the pulse between my legs. I want him to consume me. He slips down and settles there between my legs and I open to him, as if I could kiss him back there, the way he's kissing me. I give to him, move into him, and I slip down to a place past things like beds and sheets and skin. And I let the laughing rise and sweep deep inside where only blood and muscles sound. He has me. There I go.

I come back to the sighing sound of me, a girl on a bed with a man hanging on and crawling up, nuzzling at her breast, my breast, holding me like I'm a life raft, as if he were the one nearly swept away by crashing black foam waves.

He likes to make me come like that, first and full, so then with one job done we can get on to other things. He holds me hard and whispers, "I love to make you come." The words stick in my head, like tape stuck on my fingers.

I push him back, and climb on top, say, "I want to make you come now."

He looks at me and laughs. "You don't talk like that, my little Katy girl."

"Maybe you don't know." I grab his hips now, pull him close and hard. He doesn't know I'm gifted, doesn't know I have his private number, doesn't know I'm strong. He lifts and shoves inside me, and I squeeze his shoulders, pushing down with all of me and hard. He stops, holds me tight and rolls over to get me underneath. He grabs my head between his hands and stares, says, "Let me look at you. Hold still." He stares until the room goes still. I blink because sometimes a blink is all I have with him to keep my secrets back. I try to turn away. He takes me then, lifts my hips and plunges in and in again with those long smooth strokes that hit so full and hard. I open my eyes just slightly, see him fuzzy between my lashes up there so big and old and trying, not like the boys who just go in and out, while their bodies somehow hold back, faces strained as if a penis is an untrained dog pulling at the leash.

He seems something more than man, his will a larger hot and hungry force. He's plunging, rising with me his raft in his blue-black sea, the froth of waves swirling us forward toward some promise of land. But it's his own land he travels toward, his life that has me fixed now in this moment, pinned by thrusting weight. I open my eyes, see him watching the bedside table where the phone quivers out a silent call. I can feel its plastic buzz, mild voltage whirring in my head. I freeze and hold back the urge to leap up, throw him off. His face comes back to me and he smiles, says, "They can wait." He presses down, and holds me hard. "My little witch, let's finish." He shoves in hard.

"Okay," I say and I push back until I feel the shudder of his coming. I sink once more to try to catch the swirling feel of him inside me. But I feel nothing there like gushing streams, just a little aching throb. I open my eyes to the flat dimness of the ceiling, let him hold me while we ease back to the room where the walls settle into place. The heater having reached its set temperature, shuts down. The air goes silent, still. I feel the slow sleeping weight of him pressing on my chest. I push him off and over. Suddenly he sighs. "I need my sweet Calypso," he says, as he rolls on his back.

"Katy," I whisper. I look at him grinning there with his eyes closed. I say a little louder now, "But now you have to leave."

He lifts his head and glances at the clock. "Not yet," he says, "not yet." He rolls back, says "Wake me in fifteen minutes." He sighs and sinks away. In just a few breaths, I know he'll be asleep.

I prop myself up on pillows, look around the room, lie back, listen to the sound of traffic in the night. A car horn beeps, quick playful sounds, some guy yells "Whoowee!"

Outside the boys are revving cars at traffic lights and girls are laughing, living lives without cell phones, business cards and scheduled plans. He's snoring lightly now so I reach, grip the phone, press the button to illuminate the number. It's not the realtor's number. This time it's his wife. She must be tired of waiting. She's a lawyer, knows the price of time.

I scoot softly from the sheets and cross the room to find my clothes where we left them puddled on the floor. Dressed, I pause at the window, wonder what it is I'm wanting. Movies, popcorn, friends? What did Calypso want once she knew the man was leaving. Did she want to call his wife and warn her, say your husband is a tiny thing so vulnerable to adventure, a glance, a song, a god's quick breath can wreck his ship, a soft white breast can keep him seven years.

I walk past the bed and whisper, "You're running out of time." I kneel by the bedside table, pick up the phone, and punch the wife's number thinking I just want to hear her voice, a human voice while he lies dreaming between the sheets. I listen to three rings, the click, and then a moment's white noise as the receiver rises through the air to connect with her mouth, her ears. "John," she says, thinking it is him. He stirs up from the bed now, stares at me. She says hello now with the tired, bored way anybody has when doing things that don't add up to something. She says hello again, harder, louder this time.

He straightens with a frown and struggles, tangled in the sheets.

I jump back, say, "Hello. My name is Katy, and I have a message for you."

He's scrambling across the bed now lunging for me. I hug the phone closer and say, "Your husband's coming home soon." He drops back, frozen.

"Hello, hello," his wife says. "Who's speaking, please?"

I can't believe the *please*. But of course, when the world is slipping out beneath us, we always reach for whatever thing is close at hand, cry please. So I put the phone on the edge of the bed, watch him listen to his wife's voice floating in the air. "Good bye," I say to his face fixed, staring toward some future time and place he doesn't know. He punches the phone off, sits shivering in the sheets. I say his name, "John." Then his words, his language once stuck inside my brain comes slipping out as I move toward the door. "You are a vision now," I say. "A mythic man caught in a contemporary frame." He bends his head so I won't see his fear. "But you're smart," I say. "You'll think of some good story." I grab my coat and scarf, start bundling up as I move toward the door. I open it and the florescent white glare of the hallway light pours in. I glance back, see him, suddenly older than I thought. I shut the door leaving him in his darkness, know he'll tell his wife some story she'll believe by faith or choice.

I walk through the hallway's hard light, push against the bar of the exit door and hurry down the stairs. I feel I could run forever once I'm out on streets and concrete. He thought I was a vision, forgetting visions rise from a mortal world of simple things like dirt that sits eternal under hotel rooms and highways. He thought with me we were lifted up by fire to smoking air where we could live a myth of his invention. But in time it's earth that always claims us. I might be young, but I'm gifted. I know necessity of the gravity that holds us, gives us ground to walk this mortal world while we persist in dreams.

Lost
Souls
Go Wandering

I t can happen like this in the cold light of a late night airport. A man slips his briefcase between his seat and yours at the bar. You feel him gaze over the shape of your hips and know he will hit, nudging nearer, his very pulse whispering, are you game?

It can happen when you're aching to feed a hunger, recover the soul you're sure is still stretched across air currents thirty thousand feet up, hovering somewhere between Salt Lake City and there, where you are, the Cincinnati airport bar, waiting for that last connection that will fly you safely home.

You sip a micro-brewed beer and feign interest in the television over the bar where the Red Wings and Mighty

Ducks battle a hockey puck across ice while crowds scream. You gaze past the black glass beyond the terminal where ground lights glow blue and the red lights of a plane go gliding down a runway, and you feel him watching, certain he can see you wavering like a mirage.

There was a time you loved the sport of men. You went through them like taxi rides, some bumpy, some smooth, some reckless, and you rode until you tired of the scenery. Casually you'd say here's where I get out, and then you paid them as your feet stretched toward the curb. You always paid, no matter how brief the ride.

But this man in the airport, an older man in a sport coat, gray flannel slacks a bit too tight across the bony thigh stretched near you, he reminds you of something. He will move in like a crocodile, wait, watch, then strike. You are accustomed to playing reptile. Your blood is cooler now.

We have no future, Alice. The man you loved said it flat, an engineer's calculation of efficient function, weight, and friction wear and tear. *It doesn't work with you there, me here.* He laced his fingers together, then yanked them apart like a drawbridge broken. If you tried to cross it, you'd fall through whistling air.

You drink your beer too fast, hope you won't end up walking wobbly to your plane. You like to think you have more grace than that. But you like to think a lot of things that fail you. You thought he'd flown you out to share the red rock desert landscape, Castle Valley, Canyon Lands. But he flew you out to say farewell, he loved a Mormon girl. Blue-eyed, blonde, the kind of girl never bruised by bar rooms, taxi rides. He said he needed a woman who believed in things like visions, angels, promised lands. With a friendly kiss good-bye, his light dry lips blew like a desert wind, left you standing on a red rock cliff, your heart hissing in the hot blast of sudden weather change.

The stranger's arm rests on the counter, his jacket sleeve inches from your elbow. You see him point toward your beer and nod to the bartender.

You glance up at the TV screen when the Red Wings make a score.

"Good game?" the stranger says.

You shrug.

He turns toward the screen, and you see he's old, but handsome once, late fifties and worn from too many cigarettes, sleepless nights and booze. Successful, you figure, comfortable wherever he stands, easy with women like the man who left you standing at the airport, who hurried back to planned streets where from any point in town you can turn and see the steeple of the Mormon tabernacle calling, lifting your spirit to the glory of—you don't know what. You sip your beer, remembering, *we have no future, Alice.*

The man reaches across you for an ashtray. "Do you mind?"

You smell his man-smell the way a recovered alcoholic makes the mistake of sucking in the scent of a whiskey floating by on a waiter's tray. You breathe the scent of cigarettes and wool. When your heart is hollow as a flute, you play. "Do I mind?" you say. "That depends."

He grins, and like the elegant bad guy in a movie, he takes an imported cigarette from a silver case, lights it. He has the bones of an aristocrat, thin nostrils, his skin stretched smooth and tight.

You like his heavy-lidded eyes, almond-shaped, and a dark gray shade as blank as slate. "You look like a woman with taste." He grins, offering you one.

You feel him watching, waiting for you to reach. You shake your head. "I outgrew those things."

"Still growing," he laughs. "I like that."

You shrug. "It's tempting, but I'll regret it. Get home and want to go buy a pack. No smoking in my house."

"Your house," he says. "That's good."

You smile a little, tell yourself he has a thing about owning things; then picture him creeping at your window, rattling the knob at your door.

So you ask, "Where are you going?"

"Centerville," he says. "The center of the universe." He grips his beer. "But everywhere and nowhere is the center of the universe, I suppose." He drinks like someone parched. "Depends on your map." He leans. "You probably believe in things like maps." He ignores your silence. "Maps make you think you follow a little line, it will take you right where you want to go. But there are detours," he whispers.

You feel a trembling along your spine and look around. Your only exit will be your gate and the guards won't let him in. He's a businessman, you think. Just playing games. Still, you take comfort in the janitor giving the carpet his final sweep with the vacuum, a cleaning woman placing a "CLOSED" sign in front of the bathroom door.

"So where are you from?" you ask with your eyes on the TV screen. You don't know a thing about hockey, can only guess surely the Red Wings will swoop like hawks and rip the Mighty Ducks to feathers, blood and bone.

"Boca Raton," he says. "The land of silk and money." He rubs his fingers together and grins. "I'm a consultant— I show people with money how to collect more money from those who don't want to pay."

"Oh," you say, "like the Mafia. I'll make you an offer you can't refuse?"

He leans back, laughs, and lights a cigarette. "No guns, just technique." He pats your hand. "I like you," he says. "I knew it from the start."

You make your hand stiff under his touch until he releases. Then you sip your beer.

"I make people pay their bills. These days people think they can stay in debt forever. But there's a reckoning always." He exhales a cloud of smoke.

"Reckoning?" you say.

"Never mind." He runs his gaze up and down you, not leering really, more as if you are something he might buy.

You catch the bartender's glance and tap your glass with your finger for another beer.

"You would fit well down in Boca Raton," the stranger says. "Classy. But. . . " He pauses, gazes you over. "Sexy." The word hangs between you. "You look like that woman in *Blue Velvet*." He closes his eyes, shakes his head, and grins. "Loved that movie. You've got that woman's hair, those sad, hungry eyes."

You laugh. "I'm nothing like her."

"But you are." He takes your chin so lightly you let him. He stares. "You have that softness, a strength that's broken, but still alive." Leaning back, he nods. "Yes, vulnerable, but, my dear, you like to get what you want. *Simpatico*." He signals a little toast and drinks. "I was meant to meet you."

"Look," you say. "We've got a little layover in the Cincinnati airport. How much can it mean?"

"Nothing's impossible," he says. He nods toward the bartender. "Except maybe getting another drink." He mashes his cigarette out, knocks the ashtray down the counter. "I smoke them, but can't stand the smell. The way it lingers."

"I like the smell of smoke," you say. "It reminds me of the smell of men."

"And how long has it been since you smelled a man?"

He lights up again and exhales smoke from deep within his lungs out through thin lips, nothing like the lips you loved once. But you want to run your fingertip over the delicate lines just to feel the potential. He nudges you. "You like adventures, don't you."

"I used to," you say.

"You're just wounded," he says, then looks up at the game as if you've disappeared, as if nothing, not a word has passed between you.

You gaze at this man of taut muscle and bone. You can't imagine blood there, just smoke and sand and a cold gray stream of water. Suddenly you're weak and remember you're still waiting for your soul to fly through those miles of winds to find you. "I'll be just fine, once my soul gets here."

"Soul?" he laughs.

"Native Americans believe that when you travel at high speed, it takes awhile for your soul to catch up. A kind of spiritual jet lag," you say. "If I sit long enough, my soul will find me."

"Lost souls go wandering," he grins.

Anything can happen when you sip a second beer with a stranger. *No future*, he told you, the interlaced bridge of his fingers splayed open to empty air. You stiffened. You turned toward your own gate. And the only thing that kept your legs moving, your tears back, head up, was your old voice whispering, *What the hell*.

When his hand touches your arm, you feel the rush of a bungee jumper stepping off the bridge, trusting technology that of course could snap as you go falling.

"What was the guy's name?" he asks.

"The guy?"

"*Blue Velvet*. You know, the one who had to have the gas mask before he could get it up."

"Frank," you say. "His name was Frank."

The bartender slides another beer toward the stranger.

"No, his name. The actor. Jesus. I hate forgetting a name." He picks up his beer. "What's your name?"

"Alice," you say.

"Sure and I'm the white rabbit." He drinks in deep strong gulps. "Help me remember. God I won't rest until remember that guy's name."

You can see the actor's twisted face. You can see his hand hold the woman's head against the floor while he stuffs the end of a black scarf in her mouth, the other end in his mouth, and the way it stretched and jerked between them. It was only a movie. The actor's name. You can almost reach it, see it like a silver key drifting down though blue water.

You shrug. "The more I try to remember, the more it slips away." You sip your beer. "Tonight, while I'm falling asleep, I'll remember." You look up at the screen. "Maybe I'll call and tell you. You'll sleep better then." A Mighty Duck is down on ice, the battle frozen as referees bend attending.

He leans and whispers, breath teasing at your neck, "I would sleep better with you." A tingling dances down your skin, and you can't resist the warming. "Wouldn't you sleep better with someone there beside you."

"I have someone," you say. The crowd is roaring on the screen. The Duck is up again, but the Redwings have the lead.

"You like sports?" he says, watching the screen. "I like some sports. Hunting, fishing, target practice. Solitary things."

"Solitary," you say. Tears sting at your eyes.

"You should relax," he says. He gently squeezes your hand.

You study his face. You've never seen such dryness, such weary red-rimmed eyes.

"We're *simpatico*," he says.

"You only hope so for your game."

"My game," he smiles. "I'm serious. Wouldn't you like to just slip off somewhere and kiss?'

"No," you say laughing.

"We were meant to meet," he says. Didn't you hear it?" He snaps his fingers. "An instant click." He leans close. "It's an animal thing."

You had an animal heart once, a strong muscle pumping, but it has shrunken to a tiny flickering thing. And he has reached inside you, fingered past the protective cage of bone to press your heart in his palm, squeeze it down to a dull thumping beat of instinct.

He strokes the back of your hand. "Do I scare you?"

You shake your head and glance up at the screen, Red Wings pounding Mighty Ducks on ice.

He grips your wrist, and you flinch. "I just want to feel your pulse." Your skin eases to his touch. You always liked that brief connection of your pulse rippling through a nurse's fingertips while she listened, measured your state of health.

"What's your name?" you ask.

"Frank," he grins.

"No, really."

"Really," he says. "What do you think of that?"

You shrug. "It's only a name."

He shakes his head. "Names are important. Names give you a hold on things. In the Bible, Adam named the things of this world. God gave him dominion. Names give you dominion." He pauses, adds, "Alice." He drains his beer. You watch the swift movement of his jaw.

You feel a shiver as if from your peripheral vision you've seen a crocodile creep between the tightly arranged chairs of the airport. This man pulls you back across the dark line to thick green water where fish flicker and reptiles twitch.

Something at the base of your brain tingles, heat fingers at your ribs, a hot oscillation between repulsion and attraction. You want to kiss this man, want to feel his hands.

You see *Blue Velvet*, Frank shoving the mask to his face, the way she opened her mouth to that knot of scarf.

He strokes your hand. "I don't mean to scare you."

"You don't," you say pulling back.

"Oh," he lights another cigarette. "But you're trembling," he says, then adds, "Don't worry."

It can happen when you sight a flame, and see how close you can get without burning. "I think it's time to go," you say, and you turn to your watch disguised as a bracelet. You lift the lid over the face to check the time. The intricate silver filigree studded with marcacite glimmers. You're amazed to see you still have fifteen minutes left.

He grabs your wrist. "I didn't know it was a watch." He pulls your hand close. "That's extraordinary," he says. "Antique?"

You shake your head. "It's not worth as much as it looks."

"Nothing is," he says. He shuts the watch and kisses your hand. You're surprised by softness from such thin lips. You feel the trace of moisture left.

You wonder if the watch is broken. "It's like time stopped," you say.

"It can do that sometimes." He pulls your hand closer, holds it to his chest. You feel the dry quick beat of him through his shirt. He reaches, clicks the watch shut. You glance out at the dark night beyond the glass and imagine the planes frozen, caught in their circles waiting for the signal to land. He releases your hand.

You turn toward the black glass window, see a plane roaring down the runway. You sigh as it defies gravity at last, rises to the night. "I want to be home," you say. You open your ticket to check departure time.

"Can I see it?" he says as he slips the ticket from your hand. You wonder what he could be looking for. "Checking your name," he says. "It's important to know your name, and sometimes women lie. Yes, it's Alice." He sighs. "I'd hoped for better. You deserve a more uncommon name: Nicole, Roxanne, Dolores."

"Sorry to disappoint you." You take the ticket back.

He shakes his head. "You won't disappoint me."

You feel a rippling heat.

His breath brushes your cheek. "Can I kiss you?"

"No." You put your money on the counter, rise, but he holds your arm.

"Let me walk you to your plane," he says tossing money on the counter. "Okay," you say and keep moving toward the gate. There's a line there, a dozen or so scattered, waiting like you to duck into that prop plane, belt in, and trust machinery to lift them whirring over miles of darkness, take them back to familiar highways.

"Let me kiss you," he says.

You laugh.

"You know you want to."

You feel a blush wash over your face, and you stand giggling.

He moves closer. "You know you want to, so why don't you." He backs away as if he'll leave. "Just a kiss?"

You shake your head, step toward him. You feel the rush of a roller coaster, the breath of laughter tumbling terrified. "Okay," you say.

He bends, arms wrapping round you, lifting you up to his mouth, wet, soft, and pushing, pulling, more wet that any mouth you've ever kissed, his tongue lunging. You open, let him feed, and feel strangers watching. They think he loves you, longs for you. You feel your skin ripple, alive and muscled, fluid suddenly, like a stunned fish released back to water.

You push away.

"You liked that," he says. He backs off, suddenly not a danger, just a man there, a well-dressed older man in a jacket, flannel slacks, and a briefcase.

He pulls your hand. "Come with me."

"My flight," you say.

"You'll get there," he says. He pulls you along with his stride. You want to cry, but follow. This was how love was once. Love required surrender.

You press your palm to the soft pressure of this stranger's hand, comforting as he leads. And so you move with him across the concourse to a shadowed place where a gate has long been closed. He takes your carry-on bag and drops it with his briefcase on the blue plastic chairs fixed in a row. Then he's holding you, kissing you, pushing you down with arms strong, mouth so wet, you are clay, slick, spinning, giving to the pressure of his hands. You sigh, sink under the weight of need.

"That's it," he whispers. He grins and kisses, saliva slipping at the corner of your mouth. As he feeds on you, you swallow the wetness that seeps up from his mouth like a spring.

His heart beats against your chest. You feel his bones, tendons straining in his arm. You pull back trembling, open your eyes to find your arms, your legs, your hands. "Let me breathe a minute."

"Don't you like it?"

You struggle up.

"No one can see," he says, and his mouth comes at you again.

You don't even like him. But his mouth has pulled you back to a warm place, a dark space pulsing beneath the walls, lights, and floors of the airport. "I don't want you," you say, shaking your head. "I don't even know you."

"Oh yes you do," he says. He holds your breast.

You look toward the gate where you should be leaving. You see your empty house, the way you'll enter all alone to darkness. You feel the pressure of his hand, say "What the hell. I have nothing to hurry home to." His hand moves under your shirt. You pull back. "People will see."

"They don't see. Everyone's anonymous in an airport. It's so easy to change. No one recognizes anyone anymore." He bends close. "But you. I recognized you." He licks your face and whispers, "We know who we are."

No one's ever licked your face before. It's something dogs do. His hand moves up your leg. "Come on," he whispers. "It's easy." He nods toward the women's room. The sign CLOSED FOR CLEANING sign is propped in the doorway. "No one's there," he says. "I saw the woman take her cart. She's gone home."

You glance at the doorway. "Are you sure no one's there?"

"I'm always certain before I make a move," he says. He kisses you, light and sweet this time. "Trust me. It's empty."

Empty. The word hangs in your head. You look up, say, "It's easy when you're empty."

"Exactly," he says, looking for the first time, you think, truly into you, and you see something like sadness move through his eyes. They are still flat gray, but something, you saw it, something moved in there like a flicker of ghost fading through a wall.

"Come on," he whispers. It can happen like this. You don't even like him, but he stirs a hunger. With a swift movement of tongue along your neck, he summons up the dark stream running through your blood.

"I'm your match," he says.

You smile, shake your head and say, "Most men like me because they think I'm sweet."

"You are," he says with a soft light kiss. He stands and

pulls your hand, and you follow him into the glaring light of the women's room. You tell yourself you trust him, but you're shaking. And yet you laugh, say, "I can't believe I'm doing this." But you do it. You squint in the hard glare of the bathroom, too much mirror, metal, light and chrome. He grabs your shoulders, pushes you hard against the counter. "That hurts," you say, and nervous, you force a laugh.

"Don't worry," he says. "I won't do anything you don't want."

You feel your old pleasure in risk twitch inside.

"You see I know you," he says and he pulls his tie from his pocket, binds your hands behind you. You clench your eyes shut, ashamed. How would you explain? He pushes you back, shoves his tongue in your mouth while he unbuttons your shirt, unhooks your bra and softly circles your nipple with a fingertip, so you don't mind so much the binding at your wrist. He lifts you up on the counter, stands between your legs. "I'm going to make you want me. Alice." He bends to your breast.

You open your eyes see only the top of his head, thin hair. He's old, so old. "What am I doing?" you say.

He looks up. "What you want."

You can't stop trembling.

"So I scare you?" he says.

"No."

"Yes, I do." He lightly puts his hand around your neck. "Doesn't that scare you?"

"Yes," you say.

He runs his hands down your breast again, grips your hips, pulls you closer. "Don't worry," he whispers. "You want everything I'm doing. That's why you followed me here, Alice."

"Don't hurt me," you say, tears seeping from your eyes, yet wanting him to put his mouth on your skin.

His breath hovers at your ear. "Say, suck me."

"Suck me?" you say like a question, in someone else's voice, eyes closed. That old sweeter softer you has curled up behind your rib cage, hiding. She trembles while this other you sheds a gray shroud of skin, flexes damp feathered wings, a dark thing flaps somewhere shadowing your eyes.

You say, "Just do it, please just do it."

"Do what?" he says, bending to suck your breast.

You remember you don't do such things. He's old and ugly and you want out, but you want that heat rushing under your skin, where his hand, his hand...

"You want me," he whispers.

You say, "Just hurry." And you try to remember when exactly did you make that choice to let the plane take off without you.

He sucks harder, biting now.

You smell his sweat, say, "Stop."

But he keeps going, one hand pulling you closer, the other slipping up to your collar bone, squeezing your shoulder, fingering your neck. His fingers open your mouth, and you want to turn away, but he lifts your chin, pulls your mouth open, fingers pushing in. You want him to stop and kiss you right. You want the loving one who's left you now, walking those gridded streets of Salt Lake City, with his friends now, drinking coffee somewhere, or listening to music, doing lighter things, easy things, where even in the night sky you can see the temple rising with its promise of salvation. He out there believing in things, while you are writhing on a bathroom counter, your mouth open to a stranger.

It isn't fair, you want to say, but he grips your head, kisses hard and you feel his teeth against your lips. Resistance hurts your jaw, so you soften, give in, feel yourself slipping away under his hands. He pulls back, smiles as if you are a girl now. "You want me to do it, don't you," he says.

"No," you say.

"Don't lie, Alice."

"I want to go home."

"No you don't. It's empty there. You told me." Then he kisses softly all over your face. "I'm giving you an adventure." His hands hold your head, fingers pressing at your temples.

"Say please, say please and I'll be nice and kiss you. You like that. My tongue can reach all the way down to your soul." He presses his hand at the center of your chest.

Your soul, you think, surely it's catching up, is near you now. You open to his mouth, let him kiss, but a little you, the trembling nervous tiny you curled hidden inside your ribcage, cries, "Let me go now."

He looks surprised. "Let you go where?"

"Home," you say. "I want to go home."

And you think he might let you go when he pulls back, looks into your eyes in a way that makes you feel like a deep dark well where a boy has dropped his nickel. He sighs and shakes his head. His hand tightens below your jaw in a squeeze more like a sad caress than choking. But it hurts, and you strain to fight, but his hand is too tight. You can only stare up at the flickering gray florescent light as you sink at this moment when you thought you'd be coasting down the runway lifting off to the black velvet sky. The weight of the world is too heavy. Tears squeeze from your eyes, and the light of the world seeps to darkness. You pray for some salvation, but feel only the hot fluttering of something beating near you, squeezing your chest so tight it explodes like spiraling stars across the sky. You look down to see those blue lights beckoning on the ground, promising safety for those who dare to take flight. You think of all the hungers burning down there, the thousand sorrows of appetites. *We have no future, Alice.* Yes, you think as the lights recede to smoky yellow pinpoints. Yes, you had no future because this was your future, this is your future, and you tell yourself to take comfort. This is your promised land.

The
Amish
Man

B ob turns the slick raw chicken breasts in his lemon ginger marinade and thinks of himself as a man with standards, a man who believes in quality of life. He looks up to gauge the sunlight left, decides the timing perfect. He likes late summer cookouts—the grass is thick, the trees dense, and the herbs and roses in full bloom. In autumn his sugar maples will cast a warmer, softer light across his lawn with their flaming red-orange leaves. Somewhere farther north in a wilder place, a man in a flannel shirt will tap such trees in spring, draw sap, and boil sweet syrup for his children's pancakes. Some people live such lives, Bob almost says out loud, and knows he is almost drunk.

His wife, Susan, is showing the terraced garden to their guests. They're standing at the raised bed of lavender and the little crawling clumps of flowering thyme. He hears his friend Allister's new girlfriend speak in that excited breathy voice women get with too much wine: "I've only read about herbs like that. You really grow these things?" He doubts she's read a thing with that dyed hair red as copper and the barbed wire tattoo arm band. Who did she think she was? And what was Allister thinking? Divorced and rich, Allister was free to have his pick. The girl moves on and bends to sniff the basil. Maybe it was the world-class ass. Allister always was an ass man, whereas Bob thought there was no finer God-given gift than good skin.

"Basil," the girlfriend says, straightening. "The scent of basil is supposed to stimulate, invigorate. Opens chakras up."

"Chakras?" Bob thinks, wanting to dismiss this freak from his home, but watches as she rubs her hand at the base of Allister's spine, gives him a hot look. Bob feels a twinge of envy when Allister grins like a lust-struck teenaged boy.

"I think the last thing he needs is stimulating," Bob calls. "Look out, you're not so young anymore, pal."

Susan gives Bob her cool look, the one that can make strangers straighten up and sit right when she walks into a room. "Invigorating?" she says. "The last thing Bob needs is more invigorating. Maybe I should cut back on making pesto."

They laugh and move on through the garden while Bob sips his gin and turns back to his chicken. He knows soon she'll lead them to the roses, and when she bends to smell the roses, she'll start. He once courted her with roses. Daily rounds of roses. Bob wonders now just when and why he quit.

He forks the marinated chicken breasts to a plate. They are smaller, pinker than the ones he used to buy at the store. Organic chickens. That's all he'll buy. Bob likes to think they were ranging free, happy clucking, while they roamed alive. Even things like chickens should be fulfilled in some small daily way before they die. He sips his drink again and smiles. He buys his chickens from an Amish farmer and makes a point to nod hello, shake hands with the man who brings his farm-fresh butter, chickens, and eggs each week to the open market downtown.

Bob likes the Amish man, envies his clear blue eyes, his strong, clean, callused hands. The Amish man stands big and happy behind the wooden counter, proud of all the honest, basic things he can provide. And he looks straight into Bob's eyes when he smiles, as if he knows what Bob wants to be, but can't. Bob imagines the Amish man's life: no phone, no car, no electric lights. A man who rises at dawn, works hard labor in his fields, works still by lamplight in the night. There would be no time, no strength for trouble if he were an Amish man.

He wonders how it would be to live with horse-drawn buggies and homemade quilts, and he tries to see himself with half a dozen blue-eyed children, chickens, cows, his evenings spent in lantern light, repairing something, a worn-out harness maybe, a plow, a buggy wheel. Bob thinks his hands would break under all that weight of farming.

He studies his long fine fingers cradling his martini with the weight of the gin-filled glass balanced coolly on his palm. His patients trust his hands, women mostly, seeking cures for pimples, age, and damage from too much sun. They come to him, lift their faces up like supplicants receiving the host, the thin white flesh of God. Their faces go bland when he tells them to lie back under his harsh bright light. Their hands clutch at the armrests, and he sees their private clench of fear of what his expert eyes might find.

He looks out and watches Susan, now snipping roses with her small but lethal garden shears. He calls to see if anyone needs a drink improved. His guests glance his way and shake their heads while Susan grips a stem, searches for the right spot, firmly snips.

Bob picks up the brush to baste the chicken breasts lightly with olive oil. He thinks of other women, how each one's skin has a different texture, each neck a different smell. They open to his kiss, give lips and tongues to pleasure the way a girl might close her eyes and give her mouth to an ice cream cone. He knows the ones who'll take him, the ones with eyes that linger on his hands.

Susan leads his guests back in his direction. Allister eyes Bob the way a coach might watch an injured runner heading round the track. "Need help?" he calls. Bob shakes his head. He watches Susan arrange the roses in a water glass, fingers carefully placed between the thorns of the taut green stems. Then she arranges herself as she sits, long legs, muscled languid lines, a dancer's ease with movement, certainty of effect. She shifts and gives a flinch.

"You all right?" the girlfriend says.

"Just a twinge," Susan moves dead eyes over Bob. "I'm still getting over a small surgery." Bob sees her revel in the beat of silence, regrets again. He should have brought her roses at the hospital, but he didn't. Her room was filled with flowers and not a stem from him. She raises her empty glass. "I'm ready for an improvement."

"I'll take care of it," Allister says. He passes Bob and picks up his glass."Improvement," the girlfriend says. "I like your words for things. As if getting drunk can be a kind of face lift."

Susan gives the girl a nod. "Insightful." She calls to

Allister, "You have a smart girl here." She reaches, lightly touches the girlfriend's arm. "So tell me. Tell me what this tattoo means." The girl gives a shrug, starts to speak, but Susan turns. "Did you notice, Bob? I'm sure you noticed. Bob thinks tattoos are an abomination against the handiwork of God."

The girl pulls back, straightens in her chair. "What about face lifts?"

"I'm not a plastic surgeon. I'm a dermatologist. If you take care of what you have, you won't need drastic action."

"Take care of what you have," Susan says. "Values. Our Dr. Green believes in certain basic things."

"Dr. Green?" the girl says. She leans back, lowers her chin, narrows her eyes when she looks at him. "That Dr. Green."

"You've heard of him?" Susan says. She reaches for the roses, brushes the petals against her cheek.

"You remove tattoos." The girl gives Bob a glance, then concentrates on the rose twirling in her hand.

"Sometimes," Bob says. "It's becoming common procedure now."

"I had a girlfriend who came to see you." She stares straight at him now. "She had a Tigger tattoo on her stomach, right next to her hip bone. Remember?"

"It's hard to remember," Bob says, staring straight back.

The girlfriend grins. "Oh, she's a pretty girl, the kind men notice. Long blonde hair, blue eyes. Big boobs. The last thing she needed was a Tigger tattoo."

Bob rearranges the chicken breasts on the plate, looks toward the house and wishes Allister and his drink would appear. He remembers the girl, a tease with all that talk of taking risks and living in the moment before it slips away. "It's all slipping," she'd said. "Life's just a matter of knowing when to hang on and when to let go." As if she knew. A kid. But she'd wanted him. He knew from the way she shifted her body up when he leaned over her stretched out on the table. And she wasn't a kid. She wanted him to catch the sweet warm scent of her neck. And that sheet, the way she let it drop just a little from her chest when she rose up. Then she had the nerve to flinch, give a little scream when he took the risk. A nut case, he'd decided and told himself to stick to older women. They knew what they wanted and didn't hesitate to claim it. Some were even grateful.

"Don't you remember her? She remembers you," the girlfriend says.

He looks at her sitting there, so sure of herself and grilling him in his own back yard. He wants to say you are a guest here! But instead he shrugs. "It was a silly tattoo," he says. "No woman should ruin her skin with some stupid tattoo." He won't meet her gaze, those hard dark eyes as if she can see into his soul. He wants to run into the house, grab Allister, whisper, save me, save me, she's ruining everything.

"Like I said," Susan says, "Bob has ideas about the way things are supposed to be."

Allister returns with glasses brimming, cools the thickened air. "Ideas," he laughs. "Have we moved on to ideas?"

Susan grins. "Oh yes, we're getting deep."

"My job is restoration," Bob says. "I'm the one who has to repair the damage people do to themselves. It's painful and takes several visits." He waves a spatula at them all. "You should think very carefully about what you do to your skin."

The girl sits watching Susan, her head tilted, Bob thinks, as if she's having her profound thought of the day. When Susan looks up from parting the rose petals with her fingertip, the girl quickly looks down and sips her wine.

Oh God, Bob thinks, let me get through this with grace. And he thinks the Amish man, a religious man, probably never has to wish for grace. He has it, he's in it, he breathes it, he lives it.

"It's a crime," Susan sighs, "what they've done to roses. All these hybrids engineered, made only for appearance. Tight bright buds that rot before they open." She looks at Bob a moment, then bends to the fully open bloom, breathes. "A rose should be like this, full and soft, a sweet thick cloud of fragrance."

Bob loves the way she talks. She closes her eyes and sinks her face into the blossom, her blonde hair moving in tendrils across her neck as she bends. Bob realizes once again she is beautiful and knows it, and he can only stand, amazed. "You have a Botticelli face," he told her once. She shirked it off and said, "Women took arsenic for that milk white skin, used belladonna for those gleaming soulful eyes." With her gift for drama, she struck a pose—a man-eating model's gaze. "Beauty always flirts with death," she had said. Bob never heard a woman talk past vanity like that. He knew then she was what he wanted, always there beside him, and half a step beyond.

The girlfriend sips and scans Susan's perfect posture as she rises, sets down the glass of roses, reaches for her drink. "You certainly don't look like a woman who's just had surgery."

"For God's sake," Bob says, "Isn't there a rule against talking surgery at dinner?" He turns to start the grill. A flick of the knob and whoosh. He likes the sound of the gas firing up, the precise blue thrust of heat.

"I had my cervix frozen. You know, pre-cancerous cells."

The girlfriend covers her mouth, gives a glance to Allister who only looks at the ground and shakes his head.

Susan swirls the ice in her drink, sniffs it for its strength. "But everything is fine now. Scrape, scrape, all clean."

"Please," Bob says, reaching gratefully for his third martini, feels his breath come back when Allister gives him a soft slap on the shoulder, says, "It'll be all right."

"Yes, everything is fine," Susan says, smiling coolly. "What do we call it, Bob? A reprieve. That's it, a reprieve in this long disease called life."

Bob forces a laugh. "This isn't a Russian drama."

"No," Susan says. "It's life. That's all." Susan takes her vodka, drains half the glass, pokes her finger in and fiddles with the lemon twist. She perks up and smiles. "I went to a psychic therapist. She reads the colors in your electromagnetic field." Susan gives Bob a smile with just a snarling hint. "Why not?" she says with a sigh. "Traditional medicine has its limitations." She turns and taps the girlfriend's hand. "The psychic told me the smallest ache can be a warning sign. She says disease is a sign of something very wrong in your magnetic field."

Bob dodges Susan's eyes, thinks she used to be so sensible. He hides behind his drink.

"Emotional poison," Susan says. "More deadly than blood pressure. More deceptive than too much sun."

"The sun?" the girlfriend says. She stares straight up and squints her eyes.

"Blind chickens in Patagonia? The ozone layer?" Susan rolls her glass between her hands as if she's warming something. "Tell her, Bob. You make good money on this fear."

"Freckles," Bob says. "I do big business in little blotches on the skin. Now everyone's worried about skin cancer with the ozone layer thinning out."

"Oh yeah that," the girlfriend says. "And I love the sun."

"Dangerous," Susan says. She turns and watches Bob. "I hope they give those free-range chickens sunglasses on that Amish farm."

Allister moves around the table peeks at the covered dishes. "Looks great, Bob." He circles back and slaps Bob on the shoulder. "Can I do anything?"

"Not yet," Bob says, "I'll get the chicken going." He sees commiseration in his best friend's eyes. Bob wonders if the Amish men slap each other's backs like that, if they comfort when a barn burns down, or the favorite milk cow dies. Or do they simply stand straight and independent, held upright by a simple faith. Bob uses tongs to arrange the chicken breasts on the grill. The air goes still. He can hear the soft sizzling sound of flesh.

Susan finishes her drink. "Bob makes an effort to live a pure and healthy life. Organic free-range chickens. Bottled water. Strictly top-shelf gin."

"Organic chickens taste better," Bob says, knowing he sounds false. The Amish man said it with a truer voice: his chickens had more texture, taste. Bob can't quite remember the words. But he knows the fibroid research on growth hormones in store-bought chicken, the ultimate consequences of antibiotics in commercial meats. Increased risk of everything. Immune systems slowly, surely wearing down. He glances at his wife, sees she's found more courage, or maybe it's just carelessness from her second drink. Bob thinks the coming conversation could be avoided if they were vegetarians, if instead of chicken he were serving rice and beans. Bob wonders if he actually brushed the chicken breasts with olive oil, or was it just a thought. He slathers oil on top just in case.

"Allister hon'," Susan says, "would you mind improving my drink again?" She taps the girlfriend's arm. "Did you know studies show growth hormones in meat can cause us fibroids?"

"This is a dinner party," Bob says. "Can't you stick to gardens?"

Susan settles in her seat. "Women don't get squeamish. And you two guys are doctors. I can't imagine the disgusting things you talk about at lunch." She turns back to the girlfriend. Bob sees the trembling stir up from her chest, her quiet rage. "And now," Susan says straightening, elongating her spine. Bob thinks of the way geese rush forward muscled necks extended for a fight. "Now a study shows that a woman can get cervical cancer from a husband who screws around." Bob remembers tears and screaming when he tried to explain he couldn't help his weakness. He promised he always wore a condom. Jesus, was he thinking that would help?

Bob has been through this at least a dozen times since she had seen the story on the news. He crazily remembers that for the Amish, the greatest sin is pride. He concentrates on the water sweating down his glass. He takes a long deep drink, hoping the coolness in his throat will calm his sympathetic nervous system. He's seen the procedure as an intern: ice on the wrists, the throat, the crotch. They pack hysterics in ice sometimes. He wants to take his wife upstairs, throw her in a frigid bath. "Studies show a lot of things," is all he thinks to say.

"Studies lead to truth," Susan says. Her long neck seems to thicken with her words. "You are a man of standards, aren't you, Bob? Didn't you tell me once, it takes a thousand errors to find a single truth?"

Bob tries to remember a time he talked like that.

"My tattoo," the girl says leaning closer into Susan now. "You wanted to know what it meant."

"Oh yes, Mandy," Susan says, suddenly enthusiastic. Mandy, that was the girlfriend's name. Susan always has the grace to remember names. He loved her. Her face, her grace, her poise. When had he forgotten he loved her for these things. "You'll keep me good," he told her once. And hadn't she only looked away and laughed?

They were holding hands now like sudden sisters. Susan bent closely over Mandy's arm, her fingertip tracing the intricately knotted lines.

"It's a barbed wire," Mandy says.

Susan says. "Like that actress."

"No, I'm deeper than that. I got the idea before I ever saw her on TV." She strokes the band circling her arm as if it were a pet she kept there. "It's a warning. Tells the fox he won't get in my chicken house."

Susan applauds and rocks back. "Bravo! Does it work?"

"Yeah," she reaches for Allister's hand. "Only the good guys get in."

"I used to believe in things like that," Susan says. "But the good guys can change, Mandy." Her eyes are reddening, and there's a flush of pink at the top of her lip, blooming in that little dip of flesh that once gave her mouth its perfect shape,

Bob knows she's on the verge of crying. His stomach drops. No. Susan never cries in public. He looks to Allister, but Allister steps back and lights a cigar. It was all going wrong. Allister never smoked cigars until after meals. Allister's eyes widen at Bob, and he nods toward Susan, cueing, do something. But what? "Poise, Susan poise," Bob thinks, then realizes he's whispering the words as he moves toward her. He gives her hair a kiss. "I'm a good guy, Susan. I'm still a good guy."

"Something's burning," Allister says.

Bob turns and sees the chicken breasts seared dry, pink flesh graying at the edges, burned fat smoking up. Bob grabs his spatula, digs the blackened fatted edge. He knows the flesh has seared to the metal, and the breast will rip as he tries to pry it loose. He sprays the grill with water, hopes the little gusts of steam will help. He loosens one breast, turns it, shakes his head at the scarred and mangled thing.

The girlfriend says, "You don't risk burning if you parboil it first."

"That's cheating," Bob says, jabbing all around the edges of the second breast.

"Oh and you don't cheat," Susan says.

"He cheats," the girlfriend snarls.

Bob yells, "You don't know me, goddamn it! Where the hell you get the idea you know me? That tattooed little bitch friend of yours? She doesn't know me. She doesn't know a goddamned thing about me!" Bob jabs, rams the spatula hard under the chicken breast. He jerks, flips it up in the air where it drops, lands raw side up in the grass.

"Bob!" Susan says and he hears the sound of his name snap like a broken cord and for a moment he wonders who and where he is as they all stand staring at the pink-gray thing on the ground.

"I'm sorry," he says and he looks at Susan, feels the air go thin between them. She bends, her face wrenched like the day he picked her up from surgery. Susan. She looks awful. Lips tight, teeth clenched, puffy red-rimmed eyes. "Susan," he says, as if naming her could call her back to beauty. She rises, covers her mouth with her hand, and hurries into the house, with Allister and the girlfriend following.

Bob stands, his face wet with sweat, in his back yard, alone. "I'm sorry," he says to the dead pink flesh on the ground. He remembers that, for the Amish, waste is also sin. For the Amish forgiveness isn't always easy, but with faith, most sins are cleansed. They believe in things like God and healing love. Bob thinks, if I were Amish I wouldn't be like this, drunk and stupid and throwing good food on the ground. He tries to imagine believing, but all he feels is the dry heat of a summer day ending and the dull and steady pounding of a pulse against his tightly closed eyes.

A Message
From
Georgia

My sister spoke in tongues. She did it at her Holy Covenant Church that still sits on the edge of Chickamauga Battlefield like a pre-fab cathedral dropped from the sky. Imagine a triple wide trailer with wings. It had a corrugated green metal roof and foyer with a wall of glass two stories high. Regina was the kind of Christian who believed just about any action could serve as a ministry, a kind of service to the Lord. I envied that big vision of things. Whenever I went back down south, she knew I'd do just about anything she wanted, mainly because I loved her, but really because I knew she didn't have much time left with the cancer carrying on past any kind of treatment. My last visit she had one wish, aside from her ongoing desire to see me saved. She wanted me to go watch wrestlers at her church. Real wrestlers. NWA. The kind that wear outfits like masks and capes and skimpy spandex. But these wrestlers weren't there for the money; they had a mission. They were coming to Regina's church to testify and call souls to the Lord. Lost souls. Like me.

Sitting in her kitchen that night, I was reluctant, of course. I mean I like to keep an open mind, even about things religious; but the idea saving souls one body slam at a time—well it's hard for someone like me to believe. Regina always said if I could just get my mind out of the way, my heart would be able to open up to God's grace. I guess my mind was something like a cast iron lid in Regina's eyes, sealed shut to the skillet and the bacon burning. My whole house was about to go up in flames.

So there we were in her house on a Friday night, and she was stirring a pot of butter beans made special, for me. She looked up and said, "If we hurry, we can get to church in time to watch the sunset." She tapped the wooden spoon on the rim of the pot, laid it in a dish on the counter "You ought to see it. To stand up there on that balcony behind the blue-tinted glass and watch the sun go down over those rolling hills of battlefield, the blue mountains going black in distance and the sky just glowing on fire. Well, it's enough to make even you believe."

"I believe in things," I said. I was smelling the okra I was cutting up to fry. Okra reminds me of the smell of sex. It was good fresh okra, went wet and slick when I sliced. I was rubbing the slickness between my fingers, thinking about sex, thinking about Jimmy. An old friend, you might say. He wanted to meet me later at a wine bar downtown. Other friends would be there so it wouldn't be about just meeting up and getting laid. I was trying to let go of that kind of thing. I felt Regina looking at me. I wiped my hands on a dishtowel.

"I know you like muscles on a man," she said. "How often does a woman get to see half-naked men go at it in a church?"

"Rarely," I said. I went back to the okra. I was going for uniform size.

She opened the oven to slip in a pan of cornbread. "Just say yes," she said. "You'll be entertained." She had a sneaky grin on her face, not the kind of grin you give a pan of cornbread, more the kind of grin you give when you're talking about a man.

She wasn't always a Christian. She dated bikers when she was sixteen. Outlaws to be exact, the east coast gang known for skull and cross-bone colors and being mean-assed sons-of-bitches. She liked the hot rush and strength of them. She drank dark rum and Coke, and she told me once, when she heard the rumbly roar of a Harley coming up the hill to our house, it made her all warm and trembly *down there*. Even back then she had a delicate way of saying things. After two babies by different daddies who road off to Myrtle Beach, which seemed to be the place all burnt-out bikers wanted to go, she started changing her ways. Down south changing your ways just about always has something to do with a church. Her older boy was mean and wild from the get go, so back when he was thirteen he was already a heartbreak and doing time in juvy. Then when her baby boy died falling off the porch, Regina seemed to lose all her faith in this world and hinged her heart to the next. Momma and Daddy were already gone—we aren't the longest living bunch. And I'd run north to lose my accent and find a higher education. So church was her family then. Then she got sick and needed a kidney and set out to some serious praying with a prayer group. Regina had told me about the Pentecostal gifts of the spirit, but I didn't know body parts were an option.

In three months, there it was. Delivered. An old lady who'd lived a long clean Christian life died in her sleep and left the perfect gift. The doctor said he'd never seen a kidney plump up and get to pumping so fast. From then on Regina was convinced Jesus was right there holding her hand, guiding her with a purpose through this dangerous world until it was time to lead her to blissful rest in the next.

"Come on," she said, crossing the kitchen. I could see effort in the way she moved, like pushing through water, but her jaw was strong, and she had a way of leaning forward like she was ready to walk through a wall if she had to. She took my face in her hand the way a mother does when she loves you and is saying something important, when she's really, really wanting the best thing. "If you come, you'll get a surprise." She gave my chin a little shake.

Even though I was forty years old, two times divorced, and had a PhD, she still treated me like a kid, her lost little baby sister who needed to be fed and held and loved. And I suppose with her boy now grown and doing life in a Texas prison, I was the only kid left. I saw a little tremor in her hand as she turned away. "Can I do anything else to help?"

"I've got it covered," she said. She went to the sink and stood at the window to look out at the woods rolling down the ridge at the back of her house. "There's my pair of cardinals," she said. "They always come and flit around those trees. They make these chirping twittering sounds. Not one noise, but at least three different kinds. They go back and forth like a real conversation carrying on." She glanced at me. "You know everything in this world has a way of talking. You just have to listen."

"I know," I said. She was talking about God, but I was thinking of how when I was a kid I liked to sit out back and listen to the wind whisper in the pecan trees. I knew from school that pecan trees had different sexes just like us. I liked to think of the trees saying sweet things to each other, the way people do when they want love. I liked to think of their leaves brushing up on each other like light little fluttering kisses. "I haven't lost faith in the mystery of things."

"Then there's hope for you yet." Regina leaned to the window, watching her birds. "I like to think of those cardinals as an old married couple, still having little spats about something, then making up."

I didn't believe in old married couples. And neither did she. I got up to bread the okra in cornmeal. She checked on the pork roast baking with apples the way I like. When Regina cooked, she'd get this way about her, every movement gentle, so focused and sure, like a woman in love when she's touching her man. She hadn't been with a man in fifteen years, but she didn't seem to mind. Said she was done with all that and glad of it. She blew on a little spoon of beans and tasted for salt. She had to watch her salt with the new kidney failing. Her face was puffy and reddish and lined with age, but with her eyes lowered, lips parted so soft, I could see what she was once. Most guys would just see a red-faced middle-aged woman, not much to look at four feet ten and 150 pounds. I watched her there all plump and soft, tucked into her overalls with her red turtleneck sweater, her red hair curled all around her ever-calm, ever-cheerful face. When she was a kid, she had a face like an angel, still did to me, just the face of an angel grown old, a little creased and saggy, the way all things go with age. Me, I've still got the body that can make a twenty-something guy cross a parking lot just to say hello. I believe in the body, keeping it lean and fit and strong. I work hard at it: vitamins, running, spinning, weights. So yeah, I look good from a distance. But I know my face is hardened from too much thinking and drinking and general screwing around.

"It's the chance of a lifetime," she said straining boiled potatoes in the sink. "If nothing else it'll make a good story to go tell your Yankee friends in Ohio." She clicked the beaters in the mixer and set to whipping up the potatoes with butter and cream, while I sat and listened to the whir.

Old holiness churches always make for good stories—I'd been with her once before. Her church wasn't the kind with snakes and shakes and rolling on the floor. Just a sincere and tearful sermon and singing so fine my head got this blooming kind of feel to it and I wanted to cry. I wanted to be one of them somehow, so happy and holy with things. But when they started praying, asking the spirit to give them the gift of speaking in tongues, I only half-closed my eyes. I liked watching them all so peaceful, sitting in the pews with their heads bowed, murmuring. I watched, waiting with this feeling like you get when you're waiting for the toast to pop up.

Then it started. The spirit seemed to swoop across the room and grab them up one or two at a time, and they'd start letting these sounds spill from their mouths like bubbles rising from a fountain. When my sister jumped up and started, I couldn't help but stand back. It was like she was herself, but something else too. She stood swaying, eyes fluttering as she lifted her face, raised her hands, and opened her mouth. If sounds were birds, you would have thought white doves were being released. All around me, I heard a kind of cooing, and a trilling, fluttering little rolls of their tongues, so melodic and soft, it seemed the spirit had deliberately chosen a gentle language. I listened to the murmuring, the burbling sounds tumbling all around. I wanted to join them. I closed my eyes, raised my hands, and moved my tongue as if to get things started. Nothing came. I stood dumb, looked out at them all overflowing with the spirit, and remembered my sister had told me sin was a state of being cut off from God. So there I was, out there. Alone. Then Regina shuddered a little and opened her eyes. "Thank you, Jesus," she called and reached, squeezed my arm as if her loving touch were enough to pull me into, if not the state, at least the territory, of grace.

"You really ought to come," Regina said. At the stove, she forked a ham hock out of the beans to cool on a plate. She gave that sneaky grin again. I knew there was something more than the spirit at work in her plans. It had something to do with *down there*. She went to her purse, pulled out a flyer and dropped it on the table "There'll be a message."

"There's always a message," I said looking at the badly printed images of strong-jawed men with long hair, grimacing faces and raised fists. Even with the bad print job, I could see their chests had been seriously waxed. *Glory,* the curving script said, *We're not here to take it, but to give it.* I ran my fingertip over perfect pecs, six-pack abs. "Very nice, I said. "The glory goes to God, I assume."

"As it should," she said.

The faces on the flyer looked familiar in a square-jawed, furrowed brow kind of way. And the bodies, so well-made, like uniforms. Regina knew I had a weakness for big men with strong thighs and arms as big as my waist. Still grinning, she put on oven mitts and pulled the roast from the oven.

"Besides," she said nodding toward the flyer on the table. "You need to come. An old friend is gonna be there."

"Jesus? I'll see my old friend Jesus?"

She gave me a hurt look, and I'm still sorry for my irreverent ways. "You don't know Jesus," she said. She stirred the okra into a frying pan. "I wouldn't have to lure you to my church with men if you knew Jesus."

"All right," I said. "Who will I see?"

"Jacob." The okra sizzled in hot oil.

Jacob. My brain scrolled through the men I'd known,

biblically and otherwise, but all I could think of was little Jacob Blackburn from the second grade. My first crush. I loved his long curly lashes, his blue eyes, the smattering of freckles across his pale cheeks. He wore cowboys boots, and he liked to hum "Jesus loves the little children," when he got really busy doing something with his hands. He needed to believe Jesus loved the little children. His daddy beat the hell out of him and his momma was always gone. I remember his busted lip one day all swollen and crusted with blood, and other days, the black eyes. Then one day he came to school with his arm in a cast. I didn't see Jacob after that. Child services shipped him off to live with his aunt. "Jacob Blackburn?" I said.

"The other Jacob." She stirred up the okra. And there it was again. That grin. "You knew him as Jake. He goes by Jacob now."

"Jake Jenkins." The words came firm and sure, the way you say to yourself *busted* when you see the blue lights in your rear view mirror. Jake Jenkins. My first lust. Jake was tall and lean and muscled and blonde. He had these green eyes, little flashes of yellow and black, depending on his mood, and the light. He had this smile, really pretty and sweet, but the rest of his face would kind of just sit there, like even when he was smiling he was holding something back.

I once saw him knock a biker named Buzz flat with a wrench. Jake was crouched at an engine, and I was watching. I was always watching. Buzz came over pulled at my nipple then bent and said something to Jake. Jake just turned and nailed him. Let him lay there knocked out on the ground while he went back to fixing what ever what wrong. That was Jake. Sweet and dangerous. Even at thirteen I knew that mix of two qualities made one sexy man. I stared at the flyer, the fist raised, the grimacing face. "Don't tell me he's a wrestler."

Regina shook her head, and checked on the cornbread. I could smell it, sweet and warm. "Last I knew, he was dealing coke to high class hookers. Rumor was he was a hit man too."

"There was never any proof of that hit man thing."

I got up to set the table and pour the sweet tea. Jake Jenkins. That was the old days rolling back. After daddy died, momma started dealing drugs and letting all kinds of characters hang around the house. Hippies. Bikers. Any kind of drifter or runaway coming through. A whole lot of everything went on in that house. But Jake was different. Trimmed up hair, and face clean-shaven every day. White shirts, tight jeans and black boots. He hung with the bikers. Sold them drugs. Worked on their bikes. They said he could reach into an engine and fix whatever was broken with this eyes closed. I believed them. I had watched his hands. "How's he look?" I laid out forks, knives, napkins just right.

"Good," Regina said. Real good, just a little more built. Still got those eyes. Older like all of us, but better since he got clean."

"Clean," I said. "How clean." I wondered if my sister considered me clean. With my nightly wine habit and my way of going through men like meals carefully chosen, savored and then, gone. Well, I doubted it.

She sliced the roast in the precise little way she had. "He got into doing some of those drugs he was selling. Coke. Lots of coke. And you know how coke can make a careful man crazy." She gave a sigh. "So he detoxed, found the way. He's our general handyman, and he does youth counseling at our church."

I sat, pushed the flyer across the table "One of those got-busted-got-Jesus kind of things?"

"Rita," she said, soft but scolding. "When did you get so hard?"

"I don't know," I said. I reached for my napkin, smoothed and re-smoothed it across my lap.

With age lots of people go Christian in Georgia. It's the way you settle down, get married, stay out of jail. I'd always known Jake had a wild streak, but he wasn't really bad like the bikers. The bikers, they'd do anything. Momma still had her looks then. She slept with the ones she wanted. Regina, she was at the age to think it was something like love when a man grinned and pushed his hand up her shirt. So the guys were pretty sure nobody would fuss if they tried to put their hands on me. But I pushed them off as best I could, and I spent a lot of time hiding in the woods along the side of the house. I had a little pup tent and a flashlight and books to read.

Jake knew about my hiding place and told me to be careful nobody followed me. Jake liked to rub the top of my head, but he never tried to put his hand between my legs or his tongue in my mouth. I think I would have let him. And I think he knew it. I remember watching him fix the faucet of my mother's sink, seeing the strength of his grip on the wrench, the tense muscles of his forearm, fine blonde hairs glistening, and then, when he tightened that bolt down hard, the swell of his bicep. I wanted to put my mouth on his skin the way I liked to put my mouth on a mound of whipped cream. I could smell his leather, his denim, his sweat. And he knew it. He finished the job, turned to me and winked. "I'm gonna marry you one day," he said.

I was a girl then. My heart raced, my face flushed. I put down the dishtowel I was supposed to be folding and ran outside. I liked Jake, not just because he was sexy and sweet, but he had a way of worrying about me. Sure he sold drugs, and I knew that was bad, but I knew he was a man with standards. I could tell by the way he smiled and shook his head when momma once ran her hand up his thigh. He stood up, said gotta go, and left. But he wasn't always easy going like that. He said he'd kill Buzz if he laid hands on me. He said I didn't want to think of the things Buzz could do if he got the chance. But I knew the things Buzz could do. I sometimes heard him screwing Regina in her bunk bed beneath me. She would just make these sighing sounds like she was trying to breathe, and he'd kind of whoop and snicker now and then. He laughed out loud and hard when he came. It was scary, like a devil or something enjoying something like pain. I've had my share of men, and sure they might laugh a little when we're messing around, sometimes before and a little after. We all do that sometimes, so surprised how good it can be. But Buzz, he laughed this mean and teasing awful sound when he came.

Regina took my hand, pulled me back from the sound of Buzz ringing in my head. I saw the food was all laid out and going cold. She said "I thought it would make you happy to know he'd be there."

"Who?" I said.

"Jacob."

"It does. I think."

"So why do you look like you're about to cry?"

I forked a slab of roast to my plate. "I'm just hungry," I said. "You know how I get when I need to eat." I reached for the okra and stopped myself. I felt her watching me, her hands clasped together over her plate. "Sorry," I said. "Go ahead and say grace."

She gripped my hand in hers, and mine felt cold and thin under the cushy warmth of her palm. I closed my eyes, listened to the soft litany of her words. She believed in blessings. I wanted her to tell me how to believe. I wanted to know how a man called Jesus could lift her so cleanly and safely to a clean bright kitchen from that awful land of

Buzz. She said, "Amen," and we opened our eyes, and she started serving in her careful way.

"All right," I said, I'll go with you."

She raised her eyebrows. "I knew he'd get you."

"No, not for him. The thought of seeing Jake is just plain scary. I'm going because maybe if I keep going into that church with you, some kind of magic can happen to me."

"It's not magic," she said.

"I just want to feel something like grace."

"Well, we know one thing," Regina said, "You go in there tonight and see those wrestlers, you're gonna come out feeling something." She cut a bite of pork roast, layered it with a little bit of apple. She enjoyed that bite, the chewing, the swallowing it down. "I'm good," she said. "I'm really good at this."

Of course we were late for the program. And I'd like to blame Regina in some way, because, well she is so slow at getting around. But I know it was me wasting too much time trying to find the right clothes. With only my standard tight jeans, black shirts, black boots and my just-fell-off-the pole stripper kind of hair, it was hard to look godly. Regina sighed and said we'd miss the sunset for sure when I went to the mirror to work on my face. She did this tight-lip pucker thing she does like she's holding something back; then she walked away. I tried to hurry, but by the time we reached the church, the sky was dark and the foyer empty, just a table with a stack of forms for ordering DVDs of the show, and posters of the wrestlers for sale. I scanned the faces, basic wrestler types, some bald man with snaky eyes, and a Mel Gibson/Braveheart looking guy.

Rock music pulsed through the doors of the sanctuary. Regina clutched her Bible to her chest and said, "We missed the invocation. That's the opening act." I heard a woman singing her heart out. Not something I'd expect in a church, not that I've been to many churches in my life. But this was Pentecostal, and they don't mind making noise. It was a voice kind of sexy and angry, a voice with a Tina Turner/ Janis Joplin kind of soul "That's Magdelina Rose," Regina said. "She went pretty far on American Idol. And she really can sing. I'm talking like professional." She looked at me with a dare in her eyes.

"I believe you," I said as I pulled open the door where no doubt someone, someday would see the face of Jesus floating in the wood-grain. I pointed at the sign posted there: *No Food, No Drink, No Spit Cups.* I said "I guess I'm back in Georgia." Regina wasn't amused. She just gave a nod and led the way.

The church was packed: little boys in overalls and girls in ruffled dresses, and the usual hefty big-haired women and skinny old men. But it was mostly kids—brawny redneck looking boys in baggy jeans and pretty girls with big boobs in tight t-shirts. It was a crowd like most any crowd you'd find in North Georgia. And they were all staring at Magdelina Rose—a Britney Spears clone in a pink fringed halter top and low-riding tight-tight jeans printed with the name of Jesus and crosses up and down her legs, and there, just at her hip was the image of a suffering Jesus with a crown of thorns emblazoned across her hip. His face was turned away, but it seemed his ear was poised there listening to whatever music might float from the tiny little zipper of her too-tight jeans. Regina stood with her hands folded and listened to guitar chords thrumming and fading to the wailing final cry of the sweet strong sounds of Magdelina singing "Jesus lo-o-ovvessss me-ee-eee" in that scalp-stinging way Whitney Houston had before she lost her voice to the crack pipe. Magdelina bowed, waved, said, "Praise the Lord," and sashayed her perfect little booty off the stage. The crowd cheered while stagehands set up the announcer's table and rearranged the mikes.

Then boom lights went to black and bass notes pounded. A guitar screamed like a demon trapped in a cage. A man's evil laughter rose up with a dark fluttering sound like wings beating up from a cave. The audience sat silent and Regina squeezed my hand as if to keep me from running away. But there was no way I was leaving. The welling noise rattled the walls and shook the bones in my chest while we all stared up toward the balcony where a red spot light pulsed and grew with the throbbing sound. The laughter reverberated louder, faster and a red light flared above a full scale wrestling ring. And there he was on the balcony smiling down at all of us. The devil in a shiny red suit. He had a bloated pale face and long stringy black I-used-to-ride-a-Harley kind of hair, but the glued on over-arched eyebrows, and the pointy goatee had the evil effect he was after. "Welcome to my kingdom," he sneered.

The crowd cringed, hushed. I sucked in my lips, squeezed them between my teeth. I looked at Regina, who stood entranced by this man. Don't, don't, don't, I thought, don't tease. The announcer, a skinny little Barney Fife kind of guy in a black suit paced around the ring. He held his head between his hands, looked wide-eyed at the crowd and cried "It's the Reverend Bill Z Budd!"

"Bill Z Budd?" I said to Regina. Okay, I was smiling.

She kept jaw set, her eyes on Bill, just said. "Go with it, Rita."

"That's right," the devil said. "I am the Reverend Bill Z Budd and you only pretend you can keep me out of your little lives, your frail hearts, your weak dim-witted minds." The crowd booed appropriately.

I wondered, was it suspension of belief or disbelief that was required. I'd once spent a night killing a bottle of scotch with friends while we debated the correct literary term until wasted, we decided belief, disbelief, it didn't matter, what mattered was beauty in this world. I don't know which of us came up with that great insight, but truth and beauty were far from my mind when I woke to a sunrise with a dull head, a dry mouth and aching eyes.

"Security," the announcer yelled. "Isn't there some kind of security here?"

The devil stood taller and laughed. "If I could conquer your God's little Eden, what do you think would keep me from ruling here!"

The crowd chanted, "Jesus! Jesus! Jesus!" The announcer sat and fumbled with his papers. The Reverend Bill waved his hand and lights came up and two oiled hunks of men leapt up from the shadows and into the ring. They circled each other like big cats.

"Just go with it," Regina said as she led me to a place that was reserved for her in a pew marked with a handicapped sign. I glanced down the row to see what kind of company I was keeping. A blind man. A bald woman. But most didn't look so different from me. But then when a fat lady leaned back I saw a little girl with her head held steady in some kind of metal box frame. She was tiny and perfect, had a wise little face. I remembered Regina had told me that some souls were born to suffer in this world.

Regina poked me in the ribs, whispered. "It's a birth defect. A spine thing. She'll never grow bigger than that. Now stop staring." The wrestling ring glowed in an orange red light.

"Meet our first contenders," Reverend Bill said.

Samoan Sam covered with slick black hair and tribal tattoos flexed against the ropes. He bowed to the crowd. Cobra Man, bald and brutal looking, turned away from the crowd and raised his arm in salute to the devil. "Mine all mine," the devil called from his balcony. The wrestlers broke from their posing and paced. They were waxed and gleaming. Samoan Sam flexed his pecs making the tattooed cross over his heart twitch. Cobra Man strutted with his back arched enough to make sure we couldn't miss a coiled snake embossed on the cloth across his crotch.

The Reverend Bill raised his arms. "I am the Lord of this world. But you don't glorify my name in public. You keep me in the shadows, keep me in your secrets. And that's all according to my plan."

A bass thumped like a heart beat gone mad. A guitar screamed. Reverend Bill yelled, "Let my games begin." The lights went out and we all sat in the darkness for a dramatic few seconds. Then boom, lights up on Samoan Sam and Cobra Man tearing into each other. Body slams and flying kicks and back flips, legs intertwined in quick struggles, faces all sweat and grimace while fists pounded the floor. They grabbed and glided over each other, kind of quick and hard, then smooth and slow, then quick again. I nudged Regina. "Have you spotted Jake yet?"

"He's running the spotlight," she said, and leaned forward to watch Cobra Man grab a metal folding chair and knock a stunned Samoan Sam out of the ring.

"Why didn't you tell me?"

She stood with the crowd as the spotlight moved in to show Samoan Sam sprawled beautifully unconscious on the floor. His inner thighs were waxed.

"Lordy, look at that," I said.

Regina slapped my shoulder. "I think he's really hurt."

All eyes were on the fallen man, the gleaming muscles, the tousled black hair, and the face, feigning death or something near to it. Not as handsome as I'd thought when he first stood flexing in the ring. The nose was a little hooked, the jaw too narrow, and the mouth, kind of pale and thin.

It was a face I'd seen countless times in my gym, average guys with heads a little too small for the bodies they worked to build every day.

Guys in medic outfits helped the limping Sam away and the spotlight followed the sad bunch toward the back exit. Then I saw Jake. All six foot buff, blond and beautiful of him watching the procession, his head tilted with that way he had when he was just a little bit concerned, a little bit amused. He had looked at me that way once, when I came into the kitchen, wearing makeup. He cocked his head, looked at me smiled, and said "Don't you think all that black eyeliner is too much? I mean you look kinda scary." I ran to the bathroom and cried. Later he said he was sorry, said he just wanted me to stay innocent as long as I could. Then he gave a hard sigh: I can still hear it—he said, "Innocent. That's not easy to keep, and to tell the truth it's probably safer to be a little jaded in this world." Back then I had no idea what jaded meant.

My cell phone rang and Regina slapped at me to turn it off. I checked. It was Jimmy. I clicked the phone to vibrate and held it in my lap.

Reverend Bill stood grinning, ring center, his pock-marked face bloated, pale as the moon. I thought about drunks, how so many in time came to look like drowning victims. I knew what this man was running from when he reached for the Lord. He raised the champion Cobra man's hand. "Fall down and worship me and you will rule in this world." Cobra Man grinned proudly to the crowd until Bill suddenly twisted his arm and dropped him to the floor. Then with a fling of his hand he released Cobra man, kicked at his side and sent him out.

The announcer babbled something about the need for faith. And the bass started and guitars thrumming to a beat of a pulsing pink light and there she was again, Magdelina

Rose. She gave a whole new meaning to "Stairway to Heaven." Started sultry and soft, and then was wailing. She strutted, sang hard, her breasts heaving with each breath like primal things trying to leap out of the pink-fringed top. Her toned belly peeked out from above those low-riding jeans. I leaned closer. Yes it was definitely the anguished face of Jesus, as if crucified at her crotch. "Regina," I said. "Her jeans. Can you believe those jeans? Isn't that Jesus listening to her hoo-hoo?"

She turned to me, her eyes hard, but I could see the hurt trembling there. "Why is it you have to see things dirty. Is that what they teach you in college, how to see things dirty?"

"I'm sorry," I said. I really was sorry, not for seeing the dirtiness of things, but for saying it.

"This is my church," she said and turned to watch the Reverend Bill Z Budd lowering some sort of homemade crown of horns on his head. Deer antlers, I think. He scanned the crowd as if looking for someone "And now that you see this world is my kingdom, I need someone to prove worthy to be my queen." The spotlight scanned the crowd. It was only a matter of time before it would land on me. "I've gotta get out of here," I said. But Regina grabbed my arm—there was no fighting that grip. She looked me in the eyes and held me hard. I glared at her, fought the urge to wrestle free.

And there it was, the awful glare of his light on my face. I ducked, slammed my head on the pew in front of me. My breath went; my eyes stung. I felt at my temple for blood. I stayed bent over, eyes squinched shut, trying to breathe without crying. I felt Regina whispering at my ear, but I couldn't hear the words over the roar of the crowd. Tears surged, but I would not cry. I held my head between my hands, and looked at the darkness on the floor. I glanced up toward Regina who was staring at the stage. She looked more furious at something up there than she was at me.

I heard the announcer saying something about Queen Herod. I looked up, saw a big buff guy in a backless pink dress and a tiara propped on his stiffly sprayed mullet. He pranced as much as a six foot, two hundred and fifty pound hunk of muscle can prance. Reverend Bill helped the Queen into the ring, said "Can you prove yourself worthy to be my Queen."

Regina sat tight lipped, her jaw jutted forward. Her boy was doing life for killing a gay kid, and while it's not a life sentence kind of crime to kill a gay kid in Texas, this gay kid happened to be some rich man's son. Regina's boy had said the kid tried to blow him and rob him—you see how complicated the story can get, but in Regina's world gay begat evil. That was all.

Queen Herod nodded, flipped his wrist in a vaguely fey way, while the rest of his body stood solid as a linebacker.

"At least he's a bad queen," I said.

"But this is a church," Regina said grabbing up her purse as if she were ready to leave, but stopped at the sound of Celtic drumming rising up with keening calls of warriors. Then there he was. Braveheart. Or he might as well have been Braveheart, with that Mel Gibson face, that Mel Gibson body in a kilt. No one walks away from such a man. I wondered about the copyright on the name, but the crowd was cheering because there was no doubt that Braveheart with his red white and blue war paint smeared across his face would beat the drag queen. Regina eased back and sighed. "Okay," she said. "Now this is real. That's Keith Conroy. He's the real world champion."

"Okay," I said as he tore off his kilt. Queen Herod ripped off the dress to strut around in something like a pink bikini covered in white lace mini skirt, and Braveheart in a loincloth flexed. My cell phone buzzed in my lap. I checked. Jennifer this time. My friends were gathering, no doubt wondering where I was.

The wrestlers went at it. I punched in my code to check for voice messages and felt Regina's glare. I slipped the phone back in my purse, felt another vibrating call. Yes, I had a life out there, friends waiting with good wine and a great view of the river. "How late will this go?" I asked.

But Regina was locked on the sight of Braveheart standing on Queen Herod's head and making some effort to pull his/her arms from their sockets. In the real world such a move would break his neck. I looked for Jake. Saw him coaching a kid as to how to move the light.

I leaned to Regina. "Did you tell Jake I'd be here?"

She gave me a hard glance. "Jacob. I told him you needed to be saved."

"Do you think he saw me?"

"Of course he saw you."

I couldn't help it. I know what I did. I licked my lips and fluffed back one side of my hair.

She shook her head and looked back to the ring. "A man won't save you, Rita. All the men in the world can't save you."

The crowd roared at the sight of Braveheart with his foot planted on the drag queen's chest and pumping his fist in the air. "Me myself and I. Me myself and I." He grinned at the crowd. "That's right. I'm number one. Praise me!"

Reverend Bill, glowing in the pulsing red light laughed that evil sound, "All according to my plan."

Braveheart yelled, "I deserve the glory here." The crowd booed, and Braveheart leapt from the ring, shook his fist.

"See how easily your hero is seduced," the devil sneered. "Go on, Braveheart. These dim-witted hillbillies can't appreciate greatness even when it's blazing right before their eyes."

Braveheart bowed to the devil and headed for the exit, but the door opened and in came a sweet-faced buff guy in white overalls and carrying a wrench.

Braveheart shoved him. "Who do you think you are!"

The guy in white stood firm. "I'm the carpenter."

I looked for Jake, saw him watching me. He cocked his head in that little way he had and smiled. Then he turned back to listen to the carpenter while I clutched my phone. "I've really got to get out, Regina."

She glared and grabbed my hand.

"My head's killing me," I lied.

She shook her head. "You'll miss the message."

"I know the message."

"Go on then." She threw my hand away. "I'll find my own way home."

"I'm not leaving," I said. "I just. . . " But she had her eyes on the carpenter. They all had their eyes on the carpenter. So I left.

It was quiet, calm in the foyer, but still I was shaking inside, wanting a cigarette, wanting a drink. I looked up the blue carpeted stairway that offered a view that Regina had said could make me believe. I went up hopeful, but the sun had long set, and the wall of glass stood black and gleaming. I stepped closer and saw only the dreary reflected image of myself, hard shadows cast by florescent light.

I leaned closer to the glass, cupped my hands around my eyes to block the light, and saw a dim view of acres of a battlefield unfolding to darkness. Thirty-four thousand men died in those fields, and I knew they didn't die thinking of God. They died hungry and hurting with nobody watching but the crows perched in the trees, waiting for the stillness to settle in, waiting for the chance to swoop. Dying in the mud like that, soldiers didn't think of Jesus. They died dreaming of home and feather beds. They died longing for the smell of sweat and sweetness behind some pretty girl's ear. They ached for their momma's good cooking and her soft and healing hands. I pressed my forehead against the window, calmed by the cold solid feel of the glass. I closed my eyes and prayed for my head to stop thinking, for my heart to open to the kind of grace that rippled in Regina's heart like an underground spring.

Then I felt that warm familiar feeling of a man's gaze on my ass. I have a way of knowing it, can feel it like a slight pressure across my thighs, my hips, a kind of heat, subtle as a sunlight moving across a floor.

I turned. I saw Jake, the chiseled pecs pushing at his t-shirt, tanned strong arms, long legs smoothly climbing the stairway. "Welcome home," he said. He stepped close, smiled. His teeth were yellow, real yellow and his face was thick and lined. But life did these things. He came at me, opened his arms, and I let him pull me against his chest. He held me, friendly, but firm, and long enough for me to smell his faint sweat, long enough for him to smell me. He grinned down at me. "You look great!"

"No, I don't." I stayed focused on his eyes, still green and sexy, but something off there as if something had shrunk inside. I looked down, fiddled with the strap of my purse, wished the cell phone could ring. Surely Jimmy would be calling again.

"Don't be shy." Jake put his hand on my shoulder, set the strap right, and gave a little squeeze. Then he turned and spit a little into the Coke bottle he carried in his hand.

"You chew?"

He shrugged. "You smoke. I can smell it in your hair. I guess we all still got some vices." Then he smiled as if we shared something dirty and good.

I looked at the Coke bottle with what could be dregs of

Coke, but it was spit, thick and viscous tobacco spit. I turned
to try to get my face right.

"I saw you try to hide," he said. "Is your head all right?"
He rubbed my scalp, fingers pushing gently through my hair.

There was a time I craved those hands. "I'm fine," I said
and stepped away.

He nodded toward the sanctuary. "You're missing the
message."

"I know who the carpenter is."

He spit once again into the Coke bottle, set it on the on
the floor and popped a mint in his mouth. "Don't get
cynical, Rita. I know you're big on logic, but there's always
room to stretch and believe." He pulled me close and I let
him. I needed the way his arms could wrap around me,
somehow calming and stirring something up all at once.

"Did Regina send you up to save me?"

"Oh no, this is all my doing. Want to go outside? We
have a great little prayer garden out there."

I remembered the last time we'd gone outside. I was
just finished with college, heading off to grad school. By
chance we met in a posh restaurant bar. Me, with my
married English professor. Him, with two high-class
hookers. Me, I looked educated, arty and hot. He looked
lean and mean and jazzed. I saw him, he saw me, and we
both jumped back a little. In the ten years since I'd seen
him, I'd gotten an education along with boobs and long
legs. He'd gotten a habit and a dull gleam in his eyes. I
gave him my sneakiest smile, let my professor order my
wine, and went back toward the restrooms by the door. I
saw him say something to the girls and push away from
the bar. And so of course he followed me out. There
wasn't much talk, something like a *how you doing, look how
you've grown*. Then I let him grab me, and there were, hands
groping all around, the panting and the heat. And then

the kiss, more a kind of gnawing at each other like dogs going at the same piece of meat thrown in some back alley. If the security man hadn't pulled around the corner, caught us in his headlights, I think we would have done it right there on the pavement.

"Outside?" I said. "We're not doing that again."

He laughed. "I'm a different man now, Rita." Then he hugged me so close I could feel the heat of his breath on my hair. "I'm clean, now, Rita." He squeezed me. "But I'll admit I don't know if I want to save you or ravish you."

I felt the hard bulge of his crotch push at my belly, thought, oh God what a line. I wanted to say when did you turn into a jerk. I gently nudged him away, smiled said, "How many women you use that line on?"

He shrugged, put his hands in his pockets. "I just came up with it if you can believe it."

"Well I'm not a believer," I said, and I turned and saw the awful reflection of both of us standing there.

He sighed. "Well you could be if you tried."

I leaned closely to the glass again, looked out, felt him waiting. I spoke to the glass. "So you really believe in this Jesus thing."

"It's a daily struggle," he said. "But faith untested—"

I turned back to him. "Oh, please." I felt my phone buzz in my purse, looked at the screen. Jimmy. I switched the phone off, watched the screen go black, zipped the phone my purse. "I should get back to Regina," I said heading for the stairway.

He put his hand my shoulder. I had forgotten how easily people touch people down in Georgia, can hardly have a conversation without some little laying on of hands. I wasn't sure if his touch was a Georgia thing, a Christian thing, or a man thing. I gauged the weight of his grip. A man thing mainly, with undertones of the other things going on just to keep it feeling safe. "They're praying now. You should wait until the praying stops."

"But the praying never stops," I said. "Not with Regina."

"No," he smiled, and he was almost handsome again. "Gotta love that sister of yours. She's got a faith that won't quit." He sighed a little and went to the window and looked out. I felt for him then. It's hard to walk away from bad things that feel good. And he was trying. I admired the shape of his back, the thick curls of his hair. He was still the kind of man a woman could feel between her legs at a distance. I stood beside him, leaned close and looked out at the parking lot, lots of SUV's, chromed-up trucks and Cadillacs. "From the looks of the cars down there, I'd say this church takes a nice chunk of change from the tithes."

He nodded. Then he glanced at me, then back to the window. "Your sister prays you'll move back down here. She thinks that's the only way you'll get saved."

I kept my eyes on the parking lot. "I'm not getting saved, Jake."

"Jacob," he said. "I started using my birth name once I was reborn."

"Okay, Jacob."

"I'm clean," he said. "I've wrestled with the Lord." He stepped close, wrapped his arms around me, lips nuzzling at the back of my neck. He whispered. "It feels good, Rita when you give in to the Lord. I can be good for you, Rita." His hands moved up and down my sides, his breath warm, whispering, "Isn't that good, now Rita, isn't that good." His fingers reached inside my jeans, dipping, teasing to get me to move in a way to let his hands go where they wanted to go. Just the way he could tune an engine, he knew the way to make my skin spark.

"Stop it, Jake."

He pulled me closer, made this humming sound. The

sanctuary doors opened and he pulled me back toward a corner. I could hear them down there, happy Christians going home at their leisurely pace, their soft *God bless you's* and *goodbye' s* bobbing across the air. I knew they were hugging, kissing cheeks. I heard them making plans to meet for coffee, go down the road to the Dairy Queen. Regina was down there while this guy with yellow teeth was trying to push his fingers down my jeans. "Stop," I said.

"But you like it." He grinned, and I saw a little brown spit at the corner of his lips.

I pushed him away, moved toward the banister and said. "Keep your hands off me, Jake."

I looked down. A fat man with a comb-over at the bottom of the stairs glanced up, saw me, then moved on into the crowd. I looked back at Jake. He shook his head, bent, grabbed up his Coke bottle and ran down the stairway. He moved through the crowd as if he were up to something urgent, then disappeared into the darkness outside.

I sat at the top of the stairs and watched for Regina. The bulk of the crowd was gone, just a few stragglers buying posters, ordering DVD'S. Then I saw the bald woman, skinny arms, bloated face, but she was smiling and holding the blind man's elbow, helping to guide his way as he tapped his cane on the floor. Then the fat woman with a Jabba the Hutt kind of scowl; she thrust the walker in front of her with little grunts, scowled as she pulled herself along. Regina had said some souls were born to suffer, but that woman seemed to be born to spread her pain around. Then I saw the girl, the little blonde girl who sat like a bird in the cage thing that surrounded her, rods holding her head steady, with a sling-seat that supported her while her feet moved lightly across the floor. She was tiny, so pale in the hard light she looked blue, like a baby bird just breaking from its shell, all eyes and translucent skin, frail bones. She faced straight ahead, her hands at ease on the sides of the sling that held her as if resigned to this thing she seemed born to. Her mother, a pretty woman with just a little furrow of concentration on her face, maneuvered the contraption that could at least get her daughter out in the world. As far as I could tell there was no daddy around. Just a mother, a broken daughter, and the will to keep moving. I hoped Jesus did love the little children.

I waited until they were all gone. Watched the empty foyer, hoped for the sight of Regina. Some crew guy came out carrying a camera and cords. Another one called "Where's Jacob. He's supposed to be here."

I hurried down the stairway, hoping Regina didn't find her own way home, praying she was still waiting for me on the other side of those sanctuary doors. And she was. She was sitting in the back pew with her eyes closed, rocking a little with that praying way she had. I squeezed in beside her, wrapped my arm around her. She felt hot. "I was afraid you'd left," I said.

"I'd never leave you, little sister." She smiled, but such an effort there. Her fingers trembled when she patted my hand. "Let's pray for a little more strength, Rita. I need just a little more strength before I can get up and go." We held hands, bowed our heads. I leaned close. I let her call down the spirit while I sat with my eyes closed.

Slowly she started that slow rocking movement as if feeling some rhythm, some pulse beyond me. Then she started those soft, trilling tumbles of sound. She stopped, breathed in little pants as if she were working. "You need to rest?" I said. Eyes closed, she shook her head, kept going. I held on to the soft heat of her hand as if she could lead me to grace, the way she used to lead me down the dark hall way toward the kitchen when I was little and hungry at night, and she could find a way of making me a snack without turning on a light.

I'll never be the cook my sister was, but I try. I remember her last days, my crying sounds, crying at the loss of her from my world, wishing I had her sweet faith that where she was going was a better place. She believed in those gospel songs, sweet crooning words that would make you think dying was the sweetest thing there was about living in this world. And I'm still trying to hear the message she heard in those words. I listen, I play her old CDs and listen again to songs about mansions in the sky while I live in her house, struggle to stretch and believe the way Jake said I should. But who can believe in the advice of a guy who talks of ravishing and salvation in the same line.

I'd rather listen to the songbirds flitting up and down the ridge at the back of my sister's house. I sit back there while the butter beans cook down slowly on the stove, just the way she taught me. I listen to the wind rippling up through the leaves of those pecan trees, and I smile at some new pair of cardinals that always come along each spring, like some old couple having little spats and making up again. Sometimes I listen for Regina. But I don't hear her. It's another voice that soothes, and I know she would approve. I close my eyes and lift my face to take in all of the soft rushing sounds of the world, and I say, *It's the language of the Lord, Regina.* I like to think she hears me and she says, *That's right, little sister.* It may not be the gift of speaking in tongues in the old Pentecostal way, but it's something. And I'll have to settle for that while I wait and keep listening for any other kind of truer message to come to me on the wind, or in words, or in any kind of bird song. I wait, still listening.

JANE BRADLEY's short story collection, *Power Lines*, was listed as a "Notable Book" by *The New York Times Book Review*. Her stories and essays have appeared in numerous journals and anthologies. Her novella, *Living Doll*, has been used in numerous educational and mental health programs dealing with adolescent dysfunction. She is also the author of a screenwriting textbook, *Screenwriting 101: Small Steps While Thinking Big*. She has received National Endowment for the Arts and Ohio Arts Council Individual Artists Fellowships. Her screenplay, *Blood Sisters*, was a finalist in the Diane Thomas Screenwriting Competition, sponsored by ULCA and Dreamworks, Inc., and she has won awards for her stage plays. Originally from the hills of Tennessee, she is currently a professor of creative writing at the University of Toledo where she is still trying to make sense of all the pavement and parking lots around her.

Are We Lucky Yet? was runner up in the 2009 AWP Grace Paley short fiction competition.

Acknowledgments

Thanks to all my sisters Susan, Roxanne, Toni, and my brother Ben who teach me always,

To my trusted readers Page, Bob, my daughter Susan,

And to my friend Kyle, the most patient reader who can say, *yeah, there's a mess here, but there's something,* who sends me back again to track that something down.